OLD RIVER

OLD RIVER

CLYDE LINSLEY

WILDSIDE PRESS

For Betsy and Rosemary, who first introduced me to New Orleans.

The Mississippi is a just and equitable river; it never tumbles one man's farm overboard without building a new farm just like it for that man's neighbor. This keeps down hard feelings.

—Mark Twain

Published by Wildside Press LLC.
www.wildsidebooks.com

THE BEGINNING

Rivers overflow their banks each spring. The annual cycle of high water in springtime and low water in summer had contributed significantly to the development of civilizations all over the world.

Floods brought new soil from upstream and deposited it in the delta lands downstream, creating fertile new land for cultivation. It was that certainty that encouraged men to cease their nomadic existence, to settle in one place, and to turn their hands to agriculture. Agriculture, in turn, led to the growth of settled communities and, in turn, to cities.

Ironically, the growth of cities was now leading to the demise of agriculture. Civilization led to new technology, which increased crop yields and reduced the need for farmland. Land became more valuable for the homes of city dwellers than for farms. All through the Mississippi River drainage area, farmland was making the transition to suburban subdivisions. Suburban dwellers grew no crops and so had no need of floods.

The Man of God was thinking of this irony as he drove, with a companion, through one of the poorer sections of New Orleans. Once this had been plantation land, but, as the city expanded, the land had gradually succumbed to the encroachments of the earthmover. Land that God had intended for cultivation had been forcibly wrested by man from its rightful function and converted to insidious purposes.

But any attempt to subvert the will of God carried within it the seeds of its own destruction, and the Man of God could see the results all around him.

The people who had lived in this part of the city had been rendered defenseless in the face of the hurricane and the accompanying storm surge, which had raged through the city ahead of the wind. The flood walls and levees, upon which so many people depended, had proved to be inadequate in the face of the wrath of the Almighty.

Urban development had reduced the land's capacity to absorb the deluge from the spring rains. Now these neat little houses were little more than scattered lumber, and the smell of death pervaded the air. There were, no doubt, bodies still lying undiscovered in these abandoned houses and in the debris that remained more than a year after the disaster.

An untold number of people had been washed out to sea, or into Lake Pontchartrain. Probably they would never be found.

"This is terrible," the Man of God's companion said. "Terrible."

"It is so."

They had stopped at a street corner in what had once been a quiet, lower middle-class residential neighborhood. Now it lay largely abandoned. Houses that had not been demolished by the wind and water were boarded up and scribbled with graffiti. A house across the street bore ominous markings: a crude yellow skull and the number "two" beside it. Two corpses had been found inside.

"Have they learned their lesson yet, do you think?" the companion said.

"If they haven't," the Man of God replied with a small smile, "they soon will."

PART ONE

CONCORDIA PARISH, LOUISIANA

THE FIRST DAY

The woman lay face down amid tall grass. She had been badly beaten. Sheriff John Sprenkel was familiar with violent death, but this death bothered him more than most. Semen had trickled from between her legs and crusted there. Her dress was torn in several places. She was young. She had been pretty.

"He didn't use a rubber," said Levesque. "Might be we could get some DNA there."

"Depends on how long she's been out here," Sprenkel said.

"It's hard to destroy DNA," Levesque said. "Heat could do it, I guess, but not wind and water. I'd say we have a pretty good chance."

"We'd also have to find somebody to match it to, but it's worth a try. Any idea who she is?"

"Nobody I know," Levesque said. "Don't think she's from around here."

Sprenkel pondered this. "Some woman we don't know gets herself raped and beat up and strangled in the middle of a swamp. It's cases like this make me wish I'd gone into insurance like my mother told me."

"You'd hate insurance," Levesque said.

"I'm not real fond of this, either," Sprenkel said.

Sprenkel looked around him. Grass and swamp and the river, and, just downstream, a complex progression of dams and holding basins, all steel and concrete. Depressing.

"All right, post a couple of boys out here," he said. "Tell them not to let anybody in until the state guys arrive. Let's hope forensics can find something we can use."

Not for the first time, he wondered if he had made the right choice in coming to Louisiana. When he had first come down from Baltimore to take a deputy sheriff's job, Sprenkel had been excited: a change of scenery, warmer weather, a more leisurely pace than he'd been forced to follow in his previous jobs. But the job—and the scenery—had failed to live up to expectations. The pace *was* slower—that much, at least, was true—but he found himself fighting off boredom. He hadn't anticipated boredom.

The weather was certainly warmer. It was, in fact, oppressively hot and unbelievably humid much of the year and deceptively cold the rest of the year. And the scenery was... well, flat. That was the best you could say for it. If there hadn't been trees on the horizon, he suspected he'd have been able to see all the way down to New Orleans.

New Orleans.

Before he came to Louisiana, New Orleans had dominated Sprenkel's impression of the state. He imagined cast-iron balconies and Spanish moss and live oaks and young dark-eyed women, intrigued by his reddish-blond hair and fair complexion. But this was not New Orleans; it was rural Louisiana, where the Cajuns bumped up against the Southern Baptists and both groups drank themselves into stupors on Saturday night. Both the Cajuns and the Baptists *visited* New Orleans, but neither wanted to live there.

And in the wake of Hurricane Katrina, the city was looking increasingly unappealing, especially with another hurricane season looming.

With a sigh, he turned and started toward his cruiser.

"Where you goin'?" Levesque said.

"Back to the office," Sprenkel said. "Gotta get out of this sun."

"Shit," said Levesque. "If the sun's botherin' you now, what're you going to do when summer gets here?"

"I don't even wanna think about it," Sprenkel said. "Just keep me posted on what you find."

* * * *

John Sprenkel had wanted urgently to get out of Baltimore, so the job offer from Concordia Parish had seemed a godsend. He snapped it up, hardly bothering to negotiate salary, gave his notice, and packed his meager belongings in the trunk of his ten-year-old Mazda 626 without a second thought.

He was a good cop, and he rose quickly in the sheriff's office. When the man who had hired him was injured and had to retire, he prevailed on Sprenkel to step in. Sprenkel did so reluctantly but found, to his surprise, that he enjoyed being in charge. He hired good people, gave them considerable leeway, and soon found himself appointed to a full term of his own.

He had been here six years, now, and he had handled nearly every sort of criminal activity known to man.

Except murder. There had yet to be a murder on his watch until now, a fact that startled and amused him when he thought about it. Southerners, he believed, were known for their violent temperaments and their affection for guns. Murder was the unofficial sport of the rural South; on a per capita basis, no other area of the country saw as many homicides. The relative peace was a phenomenon he could not explain and preferred not to think too much about, for fear of upsetting the delicate balance. It was superstitious, he knew, but he couldn't shake the feeling that talking about his good fortune would cause disaster to occur.

Maybe it had happened already. The woman in the grass was probably a homicide victim. True, she was only one, but Sprenkel had a nagging suspicion that there were more to come.

Had she been killed where they found her? He would wait for a forensics report, but he suspected she had not.

He pulled his car up in front of the sheriff's office, got out of the car, and locked it as he had always done in Baltimore. The sky, which had been a clear, sparkling blue earlier, was darkening now to a sort of battleship gray. If the state police didn't turn up at the crime scene soon, much of the evidence might be washed away. His men would cover the site, of course, but a Louisiana thunderstorm could make short work of that.

That was another difference from Maryland. He had thought it rained a lot in Baltimore, but he'd had no idea how much it *could* rain until he came here. South Louisiana was the wettest place he had ever lived in, in fact the wettest place he had ever imagined. The rain was frequent and intense, and it was followed by intense sun and humidity, which often made the day feel hotter still. For a second-generation descendant of Northern German immigrants, it was in many ways the worst of all possible worlds.

He put in four hours in his office, dealing with the unending stream of paperwork, before giving in to the heat. He said goodbye, grabbed his cell phone, and headed to his apartment.

Not that the apartment was an improvement. He had always assumed that everyone down here had central air conditioning; he couldn't imagine how they could survive otherwise. It was his misfortune to have rented an apartment without it.

It was an upstairs apartment in a building that reminded him of a cheap motel—and quite possibly had been one at some time in the past. He parked in his designated space in front of his building—not that it mattered, for the parking lot was almost always nearly empty—and climbed the outdoor stairway to an outdoor corridor, which the landlord called a "banquette." His apartment was the third one in line.

He had checked his mailbox, but there wasn't much: a couple of advertising pieces—a supermarket flyer, another for an automobile service company, running an oil-change special. The only piece of first-class mail was a letter from his landlord notifying him that his apartment building would soon close, and he would be forced to find a new place to live. The building owner apparently thought a major remodeling would enable him to raise his rents.

Good luck with that, Sprenkel thought. He doubted that any improvements would raise the building's attractiveness enough to make it more marketable.

In any event, he was going to have to look for a new apartment, a chore he did not look forward to. He folded the letter and stuffed it into his pocket to reread later, when he had more time.

As he always did after entering, he immediately opened the two front windows and the sliding glass door in the rear, which opened onto a small balcony, and switched on a large and noisy electric floor fan. Then, already perspiring profusely, he sprawled in the leather lounge chair. He thought about having a beer but couldn't bring himself to rise and walk to the refrigerator. Besides, the chair would stick to his legs and back when he returned. Maybe later.

There was a baseball game on television; the new season was only weeks old. He sat in his leather recliner and watched the game. He was asleep before the seventh inning stretch.

LOUISVILLE, KENTUCKY

OCTOBER 1811

"And how is my charming bride this morning?" Nicholas Roosevelt said.

"I feel fine today," said Lydia. "I slept quite well, and I seem to be suffering no morning sickness. Is it likely to rain today, do you think?"

"I fear not," said Roosevelt. "But I'm told it *has* been raining quite hard for several days in the mountains to our north and east. Perhaps the river will soon rise, and we shall be able to resume our voyage."

"I *do* hope you are right," Lydia said. "Louisville is quite a pleasant town, but I long for a change of scene."

"For the time being," Roosevelt said, "we can continue our little excursions to and from Cincinnati. We've had no shortage of paying passengers, eager for the novelty of a steamboat ride."

"The income is helpful," Lydia agreed. "But it isn't the same as continuing on to New Orleans."

As Roosevelt watched, she stretched luxuriously and prettily, and he felt the familiar stirring in his loins that his young bride could always produce. Even now, in the later stages of her pregnancy, this pretty teenager could rouse him in ways that he would have thought he had outgrown.

Not for the first time, he marveled at his good fortune. It was not merely the difference in their ages, which was considerable but not uncommon. She had been fourteen, and he had been thirty-six when he had proposed marriage, an age difference that might have put off some young ladies. But she was the eldest daughter of the noted Benjamin Latrobe, a business associate of Roosevelt's, and Nicholas had known her since she was nine years old. Indeed, he had (he thought) known nearly as long that he would one day marry her, and he suspected that she had known it as well.

For the family's sake, they waited four years, but they would wait no longer. She was eighteen, and he was forty. It was time.

And what a match she had proven herself to be. How many young ladies would leave the comforts of their home and strike out with their husbands on a wilderness adventure such as this? Lydia had done so not once, but twice. When Roosevelt had first broached the idea of steam travel to New Orleans, he knew that a preliminary journey would first be required, by more conventional means, in order to determine the feasibility of such an endeavor. Most new wives would have objected to such an excursion, which would take him away from their home for the better part of a year if, indeed, he was able to return at all.

Not Lydia. She had approved enthusiastically and insisted (to the horror of her family) on accompanying him. She had also entered wholeheartedly into the planning of the excursion, adding a number of design touches to the keelboat that was being built to take them on their downstream adventure. As a consequence, the boat had separate quarters for the couple and for the crew, a galley for meal preparations, a deck with chairs for enjoying the summer evenings under the western stars, and an awning for shelter from the sweltering Southern sun.

She was also pregnant on that first trip downriver, but the hardship of carrying an unborn child and delivering it in the wilderness had not discouraged her then, nor did it discourage her on this, their second journey. When at last Roosevelt had convinced his backers of the feasibility of his ultimate experiment, she was once more by his side, a full and enthusiastic partner in his enterprise.

Building the steamboat was a much more complicated task than building the keelboat had been. Nicholas—and Lydia—had been free to design the keelboat according to their needs and desires. For the steamboat, there were backers to consider, notably the formidable partnership of Robert Levinson, one of the signers of the Constitution, and Robert Fulton, the man widely considered to be the nation's reigning expert on steam transportation. Roosevelt was responsible for building and operating the boat, but it was Fulton who specified how the boat would look.

Fortunately, neither Levinson nor Fulton was present in Pittsburgh, where the *New Orleans* was constructed; their homes and commercial interests were in the east. So Nicholas—and Lydia—did the job in the manner they felt appropriate and sent the final bill to their backers.

The total came to $38,000, an unbelievable sum for that time. The backers were aghast. Outraged. They threatened not to pay. Much of it, in fact, they did *not* pay, which created financial problems for Roosevelt later. But the *New Orleans* was launched and on its way to the city for which it had been named.

The comet that appeared in the sky in those days was widely considered a harbinger of terrible things to come.

VIDALIA, LOUISIANA

THE SECOND DAY

"It turns out the girl's fingerprints *are* on file," Levesque said. "Her name is Madeline D'Anjou. She was a hooker—arrested three times for soliciting down in New Orleans. They dropped the charges each time."

"Any idea why?"

"Insufficient evidence was the official explanation. That could mean a lot of things, from lack of corroboration to 'she put out for the cops.'"

"You'd think a hooker would be more careful than to go bareback," Sprenkel said. "They'd use a rubber, at least. Avoid unwanted complications."

"Yeah, you'd think so."

It had been a long and rather busy day. Levesque went home to his family. Sprenkel, having no family in Louisiana to go home to, returned to his office, which was air-conditioned and therefore cooler than his apartment. Eventually he fell asleep at his desk.

He awoke shortly before sunrise and went out for breakfast. He returned to begin going through the circulars that had come in during the previous week.

One, in particular, stood out. A university in Natchez, Mississippi, across the river, was seeking information on a missing student. A photo of the student was attached. Sprenkel recognized it immediately, having seen the same girl lying dead on the river bank the previous day.

Her name, the circular said, was Harriet Van Dorn, not Madeleine D'Anjou. She was a graduate student in sociology.

It was probably too early to reach anyone in the sociology department, but perhaps they had a voice mail system, and he could leave a message. He picked up the phone and dialed.

LOUISVILLE, KENTUCKY

OCTOBER 1811

Henry Miller Shreve saw the strange craft as soon as he came in sight of the town. He had never seen one like it before, but he knew immediately what it was. He also knew, almost as soon, that it was not adequate for its purpose.

His crew of experienced boatmen noticed the cargo, as well, and they took a moment to rest on their poles and stare.

"What the hell?" said one.

"Looks like a sawmill," said another. "See the smokestack?"

"A sawmill on the water? A sawmill that floats?"

"I believe it's a boat," said Shreve. "A steamboat."

A keelboat such as Shreve's, making its way *upstream* from New Orleans, was a relatively rare occurrence and would, under normal circumstances, have drawn a considerable crowd. On this occasion, however, the boat crew tied up at the dock virtually unnoticed and unloaded their cargo without interruption from curious onlookers and news seekers. The crowds—and there *were* crowds—had gathered some distance away, gawking at the steamboat.

Shreve stared, too. It was unlike the flatboats, keelboats, rafts, and barges that plied the western rivers each spring and summer. It was, to begin, far larger than anything anyone had seen on the rivers before: 116 feet long and 20 feet wide, with a pointed bowsprit and a deep draft, like an ocean-going ship. There were portholes, too, like those on an ocean-going ship. It sported a massive paddlewheel also, and a single mast for a sail. The ship's owners apparently were not so enamored of steam power that they would ignore the wind.

"Look what they've named her," a crewman said to Shreve.

Shreve studied the name on the bow.

"*New Orleans*."

"They're taking this thing to New *Orleens*?" the crewman said, incredulously. "How're they going to get something that size through the Falls?"

The crewman spoke from bitter experience; only days before Shreve and his crew had been forced to warp their keelboat through the furious rapids that lay just downstream from Louisville on the Ohio River. "Warping" was a technique for making progress upstream against a strong downstream current. A line would be attached to the bow of the boat, and a crew member would wrap the other end around the trunk of a sturdy tree on the riverbank. Using the tree as a fulcrum, the crew would then pull the boat forward. When the boat reached the tree, a crew member would seek another one, farther along, and repeat the routine. It was a slow, tedious, back-breaking process, but it worked, after a fashion, and no other approach had been successful.

Few boatmen tried this for more than one journey. It was easier to sell their boats in New Orleans and walk home than to pole their boats back upstream. Fortunately for the boatmen, there was a ready market for the boats at the end of the line. New Orleans was a growing city with a ravenous appetite for lumber.

Their keelboat was only a fraction of the size of this steam-powered behemoth, but the crew had struggled mightily in the frothing current.

"I don't know," Shreve said, with a shrug. "Won't be easy, especially now with the river so low. The bigger question is, how're they going to get this thing back *upstream* after they *get* to New Orleans? 'specially with that deep draft."

"Can it even *go* upstream at all?" the crewman said. "It's way too big to tow, even with a crew twice the size of ours."

A partial answer to their questions was delivered that evening. A number of local dignitaries had been invited to dinner on board the *New Orleans*. During the festivities, the guests came to the disquieting realization that the boat was moving. It was under way!

In a blind panic, the guests rushed topside to the railing, fearfully imagining that the Louisville rapids would be upon them and that the boat would be smashed on the rocks. Gradually, however, they discovered that they were moving *upstream*, away from the rapids, rather than downstream.

A cheer went up from the assembled guests. The New Orleans, it seemed, *could* sail against the current *under its own power*—its own steam, as it were—without the need to tow or warp it from the shore. Their host, young Nicholas Roosevelt, basked in a flood of praise.

Shreve, who watched from the river bank, was less impressed. The boat was indeed moving against the current, but it was moving rather slowly and sluggishly.

And the Ohio River was not the Mississippi River. The Mississippi was longer and wider, and its current stronger, than any of its tributaries

And there were other dangers downstream, as well, which could only be experienced to be believed. Shreve, who had been on the river since childhood, *had* experienced those dangers, and he was concerned for the fledgling crew of this new, experimental boat. Clearly it had not been designed with the real world of the western rivers in mind.

And yet, Shreve left Louisville convinced that steam power *would* eventually be the answer to the problems of navigating the western rivers.

He was also convinced that he had not yet seen that answer put into practice. But he had been giving the matter some thought, and he believed that he knew how the problems might be solved.

Shreve and his crew continued on up the Ohio River to their homes. And as they poled and warped and sailed their way upstream, Shreve continued to ponder the question of steamboats.

NATCHEZ, MISSISSIPPI

THE THIRD DAY

The university sociology department was housed in a crumbling Greek Revival building that might once have been the Big House on a smallish cotton plantation. The cotton economy was mostly gone now, and the university had annexed much of the plantation property, but many of the buildings retained the aura of old Southern wealth. Buildings that had not even existed before the Civil War often were constructed in a fashion reminiscent of those days of antebellum glory, but Sprenkel suspected this was one of the originals. The cost of air conditioning, heating, and lighting such an edifice would make it impractical to build today. It had the high ceilings and whitewashed walls reminiscent of the old houses he had seen around the area. Large ceiling fans turned lazily inside, having little effect on the environment except to lend an aura of gentility to the surroundings. Footfalls echoed on the tile floor, emphasizing the emptiness of the place.

A sprightly young coed led him up a rather grand staircase to the second floor and down a hall, where she knocked on a door faced with translucent glass panels. Having done her duty, she smiled dazzlingly at Sprenkel and took her leave.

Sprenkel entered to find a bespectacled man about his own age, peering up owlishly at him.

"Sheriff Sprenkel?"

"That's right."

"Earl Halloran," the man said, rising and extending his hand. "Happy to meet you, sir. How can I help you?"

"I'm seeking information on one of your students," Sprenkel said. "A former student, to be precise."

"Then I doubt I can help you," Halloran said. "I'm not permitted to divulge private information about our students, as you probably know. Unless you have a warrant, of course. Do you have a warrant?"

"I'm afraid not. I was hoping I wouldn't have to go through that process. The girl is dead, I believe."

"You believe?"

"That's why I'm here. We found a body. We have tentatively identified her, but we're seeking further information in order to confirm that identification."

Halloran thought. "How did you make this so-called 'tentative' identification?"

"A photograph. We received a circular from the university."

"And this photograph," Halloran said. "You have it? I might be able to provide further confirmation if I could see it."

Sprenkel handed him the photograph. Halloran glanced at it briefly and handed it back.

"I *do* know the girl, but she's no student of mine."

"She's not?"

"She was, once, but not for more than a year, I'd say. She was studying with me during the fall term a year ago, but she never returned. It was a pity, I thought, because she showed great promise."

"What happened to her?"

"I can't begin to tell you," Halloran said. "She never even bothered to let me know that she wouldn't return. The fall term began, but she wasn't in school. She hadn't formally withdrawn, I don't believe; she simply didn't come back."

"Isn't that unusual?"

"Quite unusual. She had made a considerable commitment to her degree. I don't pretend to understand it. I kept hoping to see her. I imagined she would have an explanation for her absence that would allay my concerns, but it didn't happen. It was a great disappointment."

He *seemed* disappointed, Sprenkel thought, but it was the disappointment of a man whose plans had been disrupted rather than that of a man who had been concerned for another. He wondered idly about the nature of Halloran's relationship with his student.

"What was the nature of her studies with you, professor?" he asked.

"She was working on a research project for her doctorate," Halloran said. "I don't suppose you found any working papers with her?"

"I doubt it, but I can check," Sprenkel said. "What was the nature of her research?"

"She was studying the relationships between streetwalkers—prostitutes—in New Orleans," Halloran said. "She was interested in the effect of the pressures of competition in a multi-vendor environment."

As Halloran described it, Sprenkel mused, it sounded more like an MBA thesis than a sociological study.

"What sort of methodology was she using?" he asked.

"I beg your pardon?"

"Did she dress up like a prostitute in order to blend in with her environment?"

"Oh, no. The committee would never have countenanced that. She used the standard instruments: interviews, questionnaires—that sort of thing."

"You're certain of that?"

"Absolutely," Halloran said. "An approach like you're suggesting would never have been approved."

LOUISVILLE, KENTUCKY

OCTOBER 1811

The rains came slowly, and the river rose imperceptibly, day by day. Each morning, Roosevelt would send crew members downstream to check the level of the river at the Falls, and each day the report was discouraging.

Each morning, the sun rose red and angry in a sky of gray and burned furiously during the daylight hours, only to sink into another gloom-filled night. October was autumn, at least in theory, but there was nothing autumnal about the still, sweltering days and the hot, tense nights that accompanied them.

The *New Orleans* lay at her mooring for three weeks while her occupants awaited a favorable report from downstream. Tempers grew short. Nerves frayed. Small disputes threatened to erupt into major contretemps. Order, when restored, was tenuous at best.

Each night, and sometimes during the day, the ominous comet appeared in the sky. In the town, men spat over their shoulders, and women shivered in fear at the sight of it. Clearly the comet was an omen, although no one was certain of what.

After three weeks, however, conditions on the river had altered. One morning, a crew member reported to Roosevelt that the water level at the Falls had risen significantly. Not content with second-hand information, Roosevelt hurried to the site and took measurements for himself.

"Five inches to spare!" he declared, triumphantly upon his return. "It will be a close-run thing, but we can do it! I am certain of it!"

"At last!" Lydia said. "How soon can we be on our way again?"

"Quite soon," Roosevelt said. "As a matter of fact, it *must* be soon. There's no telling how long we'll have the high water, so the sooner we can leave, the better."

"I'm so happy!" Lydia said. She reached up to hug her husband, but the deed was never completed. Instead, she clutched her swollen abdomen, in obvious pain.

"I believe," she said, "that I must return to my bed."

The departure of the *New Orleans* from Louisville was further delayed while Lydia Roosevelt gave birth to a son.

NATCHEZ, MISSISSIPPI

THE FOURTH DAY

Eudora Welty? Or Carson McCullers? Jill Winston had to make a selection soon; time was running out. She was being badgered (her word) by everyone—her professor, her thesis advisor, fellow graduate students—who felt she was procrastinating. A decision was overdue; the thesis would not write itself.

She hurried across the quadrangle to her meeting, but her mind was elsewhere. She had not been told the purpose of this meeting, but she suspected she knew: it was about Harriet.

Harriet, where are you? Where have you gone? Why aren't you here? This is where you should be!

Her thesis advisor, knowing that she had grown up in Nebraska (as had he), had pushed hard for Willa Cather, but Jill had dismissed the suggestion. Willa Cather was a logical choice, but she had rejected it. Why come to Mississippi to write about a Nebraskan who lived in New Mexico?

Harper Lee was in vogue, again, but Jill suspected that everyone would be writing about her. She decided to put the question out of her mind until this meeting was done. She could concentrate more easily once this matter was put to rest.

Jill cursed under her breath; her apartment mate had disappeared before, but never for so long. This was a distraction Jill didn't need.

They knew her in the administration building by now. Dean Alexander's receptionist recognized her immediately and wordlessly motioned her through to the conference room.

"Please have a seat, Ms. Winston," said the dean. "Would you care for anything? Coffee?"

Jill declined the offer and took a seat at the far end of the table. In addition to the dean, she saw her advisor, the chairman of the English department, and also a man she did not know—a tall, fair-haired man who looked as if he had had far too much sun.

"I'm sure you know Dr. Harrison," said the dean. "And the gentle-man at the other end of the table is Sheriff Sprenkel of Concordia Parish, Louisiana. He's asked to speak to you privately. I informed him that we do not permit private conversations between students and outsiders without the students' consent."

"I've no objection," she said.

"Very well," said the dean, clearly burdened with doubt. "Then we shall leave the two of you to your discussion. If you need us, we shall be right outside."

The others left the room, and she turned expectantly toward the fair-haired sheriff, who looked far too young for such a responsibility.

He said nothing for a few minutes until she broke the ice.

"Sheriff... what did the dean say... Springer?"

"Sprenkel." He cleared his throat. "It's German."

"I'm sorry. I didn't mean to mispronounce it."

"It's all right. Actually, it isn't mispronounced as often as it's mis-spelled. People want to spell it like they would if they were watering the grass. It's actually spelled with two 'e's—Sprenkel."

"Yes, I could see how that misunderstanding could happen," she said. She thought: *Why doesn't he get to the point?*

"Ms. Winston," he said after another moment. "I have a photograph I'd like for you to try to identify. I must warn you that it isn't pretty."

Oh, God, she thought. *Harriet.*

"All right," she said.

He continued studying her face for a moment. Finally he reached into the breast pocket of his uniform shirt and produced a four-by-six inch photo. He slid it across the table to her. Jill recognized her room-mate immediately, despite the bruised and battered countenance.

"It's her," she said.

"It's who?" He wanted it officially.

"Harriet Van Dorn, my roommate," she said. "I wondered why she hadn't come home."

"When did you last see her?" Sprenkel asked.

"A week... a week and a half ago, I guess. We're both in and out of the apartment and can go days without running into each other."

"So this wasn't unusual?"

"Well, maybe a little. She'd never been gone this long before. I just assumed it was related to her research. Where did you find her?"

Sprenkel hesitated. "On the Louisiana side of the river," he said. "Her body was lying in tall grass near the levee."

"Did she drown?"

"We don't know, yet. An autopsy will be performed, of course."

The room felt stuffy, suddenly. Jill rose and walked to the window. Outside, students rushed by on their way to class. She attempted to open the window, but it seemed to be stuck.

"I need air," she said.

Sprenkel accompanied her outside. They sat on a bench off the main quadrangle. It had rained the day before and would probably rain again today. So far it had not, but the bench was still slightly damp from the precipitation of the previous day. Sprenkel thoughtfully spread his raincoat for her on the bench.

"You said your friend was doing research," Sprenkel said. "What kind of research?"

Jill sighed. "I don't know. She didn't like to talk about it, so I didn't pry. She had a master's in sociology."

"Any ideas at all?"

"Only that I think it may have been something she was embarrassed about. She came from a fairly straight-laced family. The D'Anjous are very conservative."

"I don't understand," Sprenkel said. "Didn't you tell me her name is Van Dorn?"

"Van Dorn is her father's name," Jill said. "Her mother was a D'Anjou—Creole French to her fingertips, very wealthy, very cognizant of their social position. I always thought that rich people didn't worry about such things, but the D'Anjous…"

Sprenkel thought he knew the answer already, but he felt obligated to ask: "What is her mother's first name?"

"Madeleine," Jill said. "Why do you ask?"

* * * *

So, thought Sprenkel as he drove back across the river to Louisiana. Was the dead woman Harriet Van Dorn, as she seemed to be known in Natchez, or Madeleine D'Anjou, as she was known in New Orleans? Apparently, she was both.

But that raised more questions. How did a Mississippi graduate student become a New Orleans prostitute? Did her two identities sometimes overlap, and if so, why? Sprenkel had often heard of students who supplemented their meager incomes through illicit occupations; he had arrested more than his share of student drug dealers over the years, as well as an occasional prostitute. But usually they were driven into those activities by economic necessity or greed, which was sometimes the same thing.

That didn't seem to be the case here. According to her roommate, Harriet/Madeline was well-supplied with family money and had no need even for a part-time job—especially not for a vocation as degrading and potentially dangerous as prostitution. And not merely prostitution, but streetwalking in the French Quarter of New Orleans, as unsavory a setting as could be found.

He wondered idly how she had ended up in his jurisdiction, which was not exactly adjacent to New Orleans. He knew that tourism in New Orleans had suffered in the aftermath of the hurricanes, but he doubted that it had suffered enough to drive a young working girl so far from her usual haunts.

And if she had *chosen* this vocation, why would she adopt her mother's family name? That would amount to pouring oil on troubled waters. Why not a different name entirely, one that couldn't be so easily traced?

Unless that was the point. Was Harriet/Madeleine somehow attempting to bring shame on her family name? Sprenkel wasn't sure he cared to delve into those murky waters unless it became absolutely necessary. At this point it wasn't necessary; there were any number of other avenues to explore first.

LOUISVILLE, KENTUCKY

NOVEMBER 1811

They named the boy Henry, after Lydia's father, Henry Latrobe, who had designed the United States capitol building. The connection to Latrobe might be helpful to the boy in later life, assuming he survived the trip downriver to New Orleans.

While mother and child rested on shore at the home of a friend, Roosevelt bided his time by taking passengers on upstream excursions to Cincinnati.

He charged thirty dollars per passenger, and he had no shortage of takers. Louisville, at least, was convinced that Roosevelt's *New Orleans* was the real thing, and nearly everyone wanted to be able to say he had ridden the "floating teakettle."

But it was the rest of the nation whom Roosevelt had wanted to persuade, and he was eager to get on with the task. By the end of the month, he thought the river was still high enough—barely—to attempt the rapids, and there was no way to know how long this window of opportunity would remain.

Was Lydia strong enough? Was the baby? Perhaps it would be better if she and young Henry were to wait on shore until the boat had negotiated the rapids and then rejoin the boat below the Falls.

He broached the idea to Lydia.

"I'll not hear of it!" she said, hotly. "I want to be present—I *must* be present—to experience the perils as well as the triumphs. I am your wife!"

"The rapids are two miles long," Roosevelt said.

"I am aware of that," she said. "Do not forget; I was with you on our previous journey, and I went through the Falls at your side!"

"That was in a keelboat," Roosevelt pointed out.

"Which had no power of its own," she replied. "It was entirely at the mercy of the river. This time we have a *steamboat*. We are no longer helpless in the face of adversity."

"That is true."

"You *must* not deprive your children—your daughter and son—of this experience. I *will* not *let* you deprive *me* of it."

And so, on the next day, the *New Orleans* pulled away from the riverbank and prepared for the treacherous passage through the Falls of the Ohio.

Onlookers on shore were surprised to see the boat first turn upstream, away from the Falls. Roosevelt had decided, and his pilot had agreed, that speed was a necessity if they were to pass safely through the rapids. It was vital to get a running start. The only way to maintain steerage through the rapids would be to travel faster than the current of the river.

The mood aboard the boat was tense. The crew had stoked the furnace to the brim, and the boiler creaked from the pressure. With the safety valve shrieking, the boat turned downstream and began gathering speed. As the crowds watched from shore, they could see that the boat's entire crew had come on deck. Lydia Roosevelt could be seen, as well as her servant woman and Lydia's large Newfoundland dog, brought along for protection and companionship. Everyone, it appeared, was clutching a stationary part of the boat with white-knuckled apprehension. In the bow of the boat, Roosevelt and his pilot watched anxiously as the river became a frothing, seething maelstrom.

Massive black rocks loomed out of the foam, challenging the crew's abilities to keep the boat intact. The boat's bow plunged downward, and the rocks flashed by as the vessel hurtled forward. On the deck, terrified passengers and crew clung desperately to railings. Lydia's dog cowered, trembling at his mistress's feet. Lydia clutched her infant son and embraced her shuddering daughter.

For several minutes, which seemed like hours, the boat heaved and tossed as it careened through the jumble of rock and water. And then they were through. The current remained powerful and fast, plunging the boat downstream, but the frothing water and its monstrous roar soon dissipated.

"Well!" said Lydia, with a sigh. "*That* was an adventure!"

"Yes," said Roosevelt. "Something must be done to ease passage here in the future. A canal, perhaps, to skirt the rapids. The rapids will be a major obstacle to transportation unless something is done about it."

"Surely the rest of our journey will be less stressful," Lydia said. "I recall no other obstacles like this from here to New Orleans. The river here seems almost peaceful."

Roosevelt was silent. The couple stood at the railing and watched as the deep woods passed by on both banks of the river. There were few signs of habitation here, and the river current carried them along rapidly.

Lydia was right; the river here was peaceful. But Roosevelt remembered their previous journey downriver to New Orleans better than she, and he knew there were hazards to come that Lydia had not noticed, or had forgotten. They had not seen the last of the obstacles that awaited them.

As he watched the forests pass by, the trees seemed to take on a more formidable appearance. On land, the trees were merely potential sources of fuel for the hungry maw of his steam boiler. But trees had a way of sliding into the river, where they would lie in wait for unwary boatmen. There would be snags ahead that could tear open a hull and sink their boat. And there would, no doubt, be other hazards—hazards even he could not imagine at present.

That night, the comet appeared again. As Lydia saw to her babies and took a much-needed rest below, Roosevelt stood on deck and stared at the strange object overhead. It was an omen, he thought. He had never been particularly superstitious, but the sight of the comet filled him with a sense of dread that he could not explain.

NATCHEZ, MISSISSIPPI

THE FOURTH DAY

Suddenly, Jill Winston thought, the apartment was strangely empty.

Harriet had not been a close friend. They had coexisted peacefully enough, but there had been no sharing of confidences, no late-night study sessions spiced with giggles and popcorn and gossip, no intimate revelations about lost loves and secret ambitions. They had, Jill now realized, been as much strangers as if they had merely passed in the hall.

This had not been a matter of concern before; Harriet was always around—well, *frequently* around—and the prospect for a closer relationship always seemed a possibility. It had not occurred to Jill that such an opportunity might be lost. They had, after all, been cordial companions for two years.

But Harriet was dead. She had been murdered, and although the sheriff had not said it in so many words, it was clear she had been beaten and raped as well. The knowledge filled Jill with a deep sense of loss, almost as if they *had* been intimates.

She stood in the middle of her tiny living room and looked about her, seeking a sign of Harriet's existence, and discovered with dismay that there were none. Where were the books, the lecture notes, the flotsam and jetsam of academic life? The CDs and DVDs? She realized that she knew nothing of Harriet's tastes in music, or movies, or literature, or indeed, if she cared for such things. It occurred to her abruptly that she had really not known her roommate at all.

The police had searched Harriet's bedroom thoroughly and had removed a number of items, but those items were also of a remarkably impersonal nature. Jill stood at Harriet's bedroom doorway and looked vainly for something by which to remember her, but she could see nothing that fit the description. The police had taken her laptop computer but little else. The room was bereft even of family photographs.

Which, now that she thought of it, was odd.

There *had* been a photograph, she remembered. It had been in a cheap plastic frame, and it had sat on her desk next to her computer.

There had been a rather severe-looking older couple, a girl who appeared to be in her early teens, and a boy who looked to be a few years older. The boy and girl seemed to be doing their best to smile, but Jill had the sense that it had required some effort on their part. Jill had asked if the people in the photograph were family, and Harriet had said yes: that she was the girl, that the older couple were her parents, and that the boy was her brother. She hadn't volunteered anything more than that, and Jill hadn't felt comfortable pursuing the matter.

But there had been something about the photograph that had stayed in her mind, if only she could recall what it had been. In any event, the photograph wasn't there any longer; she assumed the police had taken it to aid them in their investigation.

On television, investigators always seemed to be stretching yellow plastic tape around crime scenes, but there was none to bar entrance to Harriet's room. Of course, Harriet had not been killed in her apartment.

Jill still felt some reluctance to enter the room. But perhaps if she had done so during the weeks when Harriet went missing—had been *nosier*—she would have noticed something that could have prevented Harriet's death. She might, at least, have suspected that something was wrong. Even now, she might detect something that the police had missed, something that would make sense to her when it did not make sense to them.

Harriet could hardly protest this invasion of her privacy, and if something she found would be of significance to the police, it might help them find her killer. Jill admitted to herself also that she would not be disappointed to find something that would persuade that young sheriff to pay a return visit.

Harriet, forgive me, she thought. Then she squared her shoulders and entered the room.

She tried to organize her search systematically. After debating with herself for a while, she began with the bookshelves. There were the usual sociological studies, which, after riffling the pages in the hope that a note of some sort might have been secreted there, she found uninteresting. Next she turned to music, where she discovered that Harriet had a previously undisclosed infatuation with hip hop and baroque music—a combination Jill found difficult to fathom.

Next she turned to clothing. Rummaging through drawers she found an odd assortment of lingerie—white cotton panties next to items that seemed to have come from Frederick's of Hollywood: thongs and teddies and *bustiers*, and a bra and crotchless-panty set studded with rhinestones. Curious.

Jill sat down heavily on the bed and tried to absorb this new revelation. It depicted someone unlike the young woman she had lived with for two years. She had never seen Harriet wearing any of this apparel. And yet she had no doubt that it belonged to her. Why had she been unaware of it?

Well, of course, Harriet hadn't worn it around the apartment; the effect would have been lost on Jill. Harriet often had left the apartment—on her way to class, ostensibly—carrying extra clothing in a gym bag. Jill had assumed she planned to stop at the student gym for an exercise session before coming home after class. But this was not the sort of workout Jill had envisioned.

The police must have seen these items during their search, and it would have confirmed their opinion about Harriet's activities. Against her will, Jill was forced to reconsider her impression of her roommate, as well.

Could Harriet truly have been moonlighting as a prostitute? And if so, why? Certainly not for the money; her family provided well for her, and she had no need for the income.

For the thrill of doing something illicit? Was she somehow addicted to sex? Was she unconsciously attempting to humiliate her family? She knew, from Harriet's occasional comments, that they were quite conservative, but she could think of nothing that Harriet had ever said or done that would lead her to believe she would deliberately attempt to harm them.

She turned to Harriet's desk and been looking through the file drawer. It was unhelpful. There were few file folders, and they were largely empty. Presumably, the police had been though them already in search of information about Harriet's little sideline.

That left the desktop computer in the living room, where Harriet had printed the final copies of her research papers, and which had not been removed. This was odd, Jill thought. She realized, suddenly, that the police had not known that it belonged to Harriet, also.

She turned it on and waited impatiently for it to boot up. Finally the familiar Windows screen appeared, and she opened the "My Documents" folder.

Nothing.

She had anticipated that any relevant files might be encrypted, but it had not occurred to her that there would be nothing at all. It appeared, at first glance, that the computer's storage media were blank slates. Was it possible that Harriet had never made a single entry?

No, Jill concluded, it wasn't possible. Whatever else Harriet might have been, she was also a graduate student. Access to a computer would be essential for a graduate student, especially in the social sciences. It was *not* possible, therefore, that Harriet's computer files were empty.

So there had to be data, and unless the disk had been scrubbed by an expert, it had to be here. All she had to do was find it.

LOUISVILLE, KENTUCKY

DECEMBER 1811

Ten miles per hour!

The capabilities of Roosevelt's steamboat astonished everyone, not least among them Roosevelt himself. True, this was its downstream speed; upstream it moved rather more laboriously. But it moved in both directions without the need for strong-backed crewmen poling and warping against the current; rather it traveled, literally, under its own steam! Roosevelt was greeted with accolades at every stop.

Roosevelt was troubled, nonetheless. The boat's performance, though unparalleled, was still anemic enough to cause serious doubts in his own mind about its ability to handle the Mississippi, where the current—and the hazards—would be much greater.

The ultimate test was coming soon. They were approaching the mouth of the river. The Mississippi, and new unanticipated problems, lay ahead.

Only a few miles below the mouth of the Ohio River, on the western bank of the Mississippi, lay the small settlement of New Madrid. Originally intended to be the nucleus of a new colony that would establish Spanish hegemony west of the Mississippi, it had gradually been transformed—as frontier settlements often were—into a polyglot mix of people from many nations, centered on a trading post that dealt with all. The Spaniards were unprepared for this and eventually had thrown up their hands in frustration and essentially abandoned the colony to the Americans.

In the early morning hours of December 15, the residents of this little frontier community were rolled out of their beds—literally—by a great crashing and shaking. The earth beneath their feet, normally so firm and stable, began rolling like the ocean.

Gigantic heaving billows moved like tidal waves across the land. They drained lakes that had existed for centuries and created new lakes where none had been before. Cliffs crumbled into the river, trees were uprooted, and houses were split into kindling. Trees that had lain undisturbed on the river bed for many years were suddenly spit up to the surface. Islands disappeared; new islands replaced them.

The passengers and crew of the New Orleans were unaware of the earthquake, perhaps because the noise and vibrations of their steamboat's own making had disguised the tremors. They steamed obliviously from the mouth of the Ohio into the turbulent Mississippi and were confronted with catastrophe on every side. Trees—in some cases entire trees—floated with the current. The flotsam of smashed flatboats joined the torrent of debris that surrounded them.

"The river is always laden with obstacles," said the captain. "But this…" He did not complete the sentence because he was forced to maneuver suddenly to avoid colliding with a massive hickory tree trunk that had appeared off his bow.

"I thought earthquakes occurred along coastlines," said Roosevelt. "We must be five-hundred miles or more from the nearest salt water."

"Nonetheless, I believe we're seeing one now," said the captain.

As if in response, the tremors began again. The horrified crew watched as nearby cliffs shook like jelly and crumbled into the water.

The New Orleans was larger than any other vessel on the river, but it was not indestructible. With darkness rapidly approaching, and the river strewn with dangerous debris, it was decided to tie up early and await the dawn.

But not just anywhere.

"The way those cliffs keep crumbling into the river, I don't dare tie up along the shore," the captain told Roosevelt. "We might not have a shoreline by morning."

"What do you suggest?" Roosevelt said with a worried frown.

"Let's tie up on the river side of one of those islands in mid-stream," the captain said. "The island might offer some protection from all this debris."

The New Orleans tied off, as the captain had wanted, on the down-river side of an out-of-the-way island. The passengers and crew, nevertheless, slept very little that night. The sound of objects crashing into the hull—some small, some not—continued until dawn. And in the morning, a strange sight greeted them as they came on deck.

The island was gone.

"We must have slipped our moorings last night," Roosevelt said. "We have drifted downstream with the current."

The captain shook his head and pointed, instead, at the riverbank and at a number of familiar landmarks that still remained.

"That's the same cliff that we saw yesterday," he said. "And we're still tied to a tree. It's just that the tree's under water now. We ain't moved. The island sank "

The captain's decision to leave this spot, and quickly, was unopposed. The New Orleans steamed cautiously to the middle of the channel—as nearly as that could be determined under the circumstances—and began feeling its way downstream through the debris.

At New Madrid, the passengers and crew encountered even more staggering devastation. The earthquake, they learned later, was one of the worst ever to occur on the North American continent. It rang church bells as far away as Boston and produced swells in the Atlantic Ocean, more than a thousand miles away. New Madrid was at the epicenter.

The passengers and crew of the New Orleans were unaware of this information, but they were nonetheless astounded at the spectacle that presented itself.

"It looks like half the town is gone," said the captain. "Never seen anything like it."

Roosevelt saw the burning houses and the gaunt and ragged survivors huddled on the riverbank. In their desperation, they were unimpressed with the appearance of a steamboat in their midst—an appearance that had evoked curiosity and wonder in every other town they had visited. The denizens of New Madrid saw only one thing: salvation. They called desperately from the riverbank.

"Take us with you!"

Lydia heard the anguished cries, and they touched her heart.

"We must help them!" she said. "We have room for some additional passengers."

"But not for all of them," said the captain. "How would you choose among them? Who would come, and who would stay? Would you break up families, separate mothers and children?"

"He has a point, dear," Roosevelt said.

"Surely there's a way," she said. "We might take only those in dire need."

"No, ma'am," the captain said. "How would we determine whose need was greatest, where everyone is homeless? Once we let out our gangplank we would quickly be overwhelmed. I'll not put in here. They are too many; we can't fight them, and they would swamp the boat."

"But surely…"

"No, ma'am," said the captain. "And there's also the problem of provisions. We're still nearly two weeks from Natchez, and we may have to skimp on food just to feed ourselves for that long. There's no way we could accommodate that mob. I feel for these people, too, but I'll not put in here."

The boat continued downstream to New Orleans without stopping at New Madrid.

CONCORDIA PARISH

THE FIFTH DAY

The yellow tape had not been removed, but it had suffered the ravages of weather. It lay tattered on the ground in places, hanging listlessly from tree limbs elsewhere.

It didn't matter anymore, Sprenkel thought, as he surveyed the scene where the girl's body had been found. There was nothing more that the place could tell them now, and it had told them damn little in the first place. The state's people had been over the scene several times with hardly more success than his own inexperienced people.

Still, the location haunted him for reasons he could not discern. He walked the scene now with one of the state investigators in what he suspected was a forlorn hope.

"She wasn't killed here, you know," Clarence Bouchard, the investigator, said. He was a big man with big hands, who looked more like a construction worker than a forensic specialist. But his reputation in the field had preceded him, Sprenkel knew.

"I sort of figured that," Sprenkel said. "There weren't any signs of a struggle or a beating here, and she was pretty beat-up. I wonder how she got here, though."

"Wondered that myself. No tire tracks or footprints, and the ground's pretty soft," said the investigator. "Hard to imagine how they got her so far from the road without leaving signs."

"Could they have dropped her here? By plane, for instance?"

Bouchard considered. "That would fit with the marks on the body. Unusual MO, though. I don't think I've ever seen that."

"Who would do that?" Sprenkel said. "And why?"

"Exactly," Bouchard said. "Don't make sense to me. Most killers ain't as inventive as all that. And this looks like a crime of passion, too. People who kill on the spur of the moment ain't likely to spend much time and effort and money disposing of the body—especially when the body ain't really disposed of at all. They must of known she'd be found out here. People are always using these levees—for picnics, for fishing, just for walks."

Sprenkel looked around once more, hoping that something out of the ordinary would occur to him. It did not, but he had not expected that it would. The geography here, even after six years, was still foreign to him, and he suspected it would always be so.

"Wonder where they got the plane," he said. "If that's what they did."

"The real question is where they took off from," Bouchard said. "You'd want to do it at night, but you wouldn't want to leave from some crowded airport. You haul a body out to a plane in full view of an airport ground crew and somebody's going to remember."

"Rules out Baton Rouge and New Orleans."

"And Jackson and probably Natchez, as well," Bouchard said. "It might also rule out some of these little air parks around here. There's lots of little airfields around that are unmanned after dark, but the owners live nearby, most of them. They'd know, most likely, if somebody took off without telling them about it. If nothing else, they'd want to be reimbursed for the gas."

Sprenkel considered this. The airfield didn't have to be in his jurisdiction. It could be anywhere in a reasonable flying radius—say a hundred miles or so in a light plane. That would enable the killer to take off, make the dump, and get back to the airfield before dawn.

Killers, actually. He realized suddenly that it would be a difficult job for a single man to pull off—to kill the girl, load her into a vehicle, transfer her body to an aircraft, fly her to this spot, throw her out, and return within the space of a few hours.

So perhaps, since so much coordination and planning was involved, it wasn't a crime of passion at all, despite indications to the contrary.

Perhaps the killers regarded rape as simply an extra benefit. In New Orleans, they would call it *"lagniappe,"* just a little something extra, like a baker's dozen, or the cheap little toy tucked in the Crackerjacks box. A reward for a job well done.

A line from an old nursery rhyme came into his head unbidden:
He stuck in his thumb and pulled out a plum and thought "what a good boy am I."

* * * *

He returned to his office, driving slowly, considering the peculiarities of the case. Why had she been deposited on a *levee* in his jurisdiction, like so much rubbish? How had she gotten to her final resting place without leaving footprints—either her own or those of the man who had carried her there?

He had heard several theories by now, but few of them made sense to him. One theory that had gained popularity with his staff was that the girl's body had been dropped from a hot air balloon. That was Levesque's favorite theory, but Sprenkel tended to discount it. A hot air balloon would be quiet, but it would be no less conspicuous for all that, and it would be difficult to put it where the killer wanted. Balloons were at the mercy of the prevailing winds. And hot air balloons required propane burners. He suspected someone locally would have seen a sudden burst of flame in the sky and wondered about it. The drone of an aircraft engine would be more common and therefore less noticeable.

He made a note to have someone make calls to neighboring jurisdictions. A systematic inquiry concerning night flights from private airfields might turn up something.

He mentioned this to Levesque.

"I'll get on it," Levesque said. "Want me to check in Mississippi, too? It's no big deal to take off from across the river, after all. That would be my guess—the killer took off from Mississippi somewhere. The girl was in school over there, after all."

"Good point," Sprenkel said. "I'd limit the search to about a hundred miles or so, at least for the first time around. If we have to widen the search later, we can do that. But my guess is that he took off from someplace closer."

"You know I've been wondering," Levesque said as he turned to go. "Is this case really worth all this trouble? I mean, one dead hooker out of hundreds. Who's gonna care?"

"She had a family," Sprenkel said evenly. "They would care."

After Levesque had gone, Sprenkel thought again about the dead girl. Someone would have to notify her parents, and he supposed that job fell to him.

Reluctantly, he placed a call to the university in Natchez, seeking an address for the girl's family. It took some time to convince the bureaucrat in the registrar's office that he was, in fact, a law enforcement official, despite the fact that he had been there in person only the previous day. Eventually he was turned over to someone who had the authority to release the information to him—an address and telephone number in Memphis.

The telephone number had been disconnected.

Rather than drive to Memphis on what might be a wild goose chase, he called the girl's roommate. Perhaps she would have more recent—and accurate—information.

He half expected to get an answering machine, but she startled him by answering, breathlessly on the first ring.

"Sheriff?"

"Sprenkel, yes. How did you…"

"Caller ID," she said, amused. "Every woman should have it. You wouldn't believe how many annoying calls I receive."

Actually, Sprenkel thought, he probably would. Most of those calls, he suspected, would be from young men. Under other circumstances—and if he were younger—he might have been one of them.

"I've been trying to reach your roommate's parents," he said, trying to be as straightforward as possible. "I got an address and phone number from university admissions, but the phone doesn't answer. I thought maybe you would have more recent information."

"I'll give you what I have," she said. Was there a note of… what, disappointment… in her voice? He heard her put down the phone while she rummaged for her notes. She was gone for quite some time.

"This is what I have," she said when she returned. She rattled off the same number he had gotten from the university.

"That's the number I have, too," Sprenkel said. "You don't have anything more recent?"

"Sorry."

"All right. Thanks anyway. I guess I'll have to drive up there and try to find them in person. I appreciate your looking it up for me."

"Sheriff," she said before he could hang up. "Would you be going up there today?"

"Soon as I can get away, I expect. Why?"

"I wonder if you could stop by here for a minute. It would be on your way."

Memphis *was* across the river, after all.

"I guess so," he said. "I've got a few matters to clear up here before I can leave. Would noon be okay with you?"

"I'll be waiting."

After dealing with the pressing business on his desk, it was closer to one before Sprenkel finally got away from his office. When he pulled up outside Jill Winston's apartment, however, he was surprised to find her waiting for him out in front.

"Thank you for coming," she said.

"I was later getting away than I expected. I wasn't sure you'd still be waiting."

"I'm working on my thesis so I'm home most of the time these days," she said. "Come on upstairs. There's something I'd like for you to see."

In her apartment she showed him the computer.

"This is Harriet's computer; not mine," she said. "I was surprised that the police hadn't taken it, but I suppose they didn't realize it belonged to her."

"Maybe so. This isn't my jurisdiction, so my people weren't in charge of the investigation here. Anything interesting on it?"

"That's the odd thing," she said. "There's *nothing* on it at all, as far as I can tell. Don't you think that's strange?"

"A little. Are you sure she used it? She also had a laptop, after all."

"I sometimes saw her working on it, which is why I started exploring. It boots up fine, but there are no files listed, aside from the operating system and a couple of applications."

"That *is* a bit unusual," he said. He sat at the computer and explored for himself, confirming what the girl had told him.

"What should I do?" she said. "Do you suppose *you* could get something out of it?"

"As I said, I'm out of my jurisdiction here. I don't have the expertise myself, and I doubt that the local police would look kindly on my removing evidence. Why don't you call the Natchez police? If they don't have someone on their staff who can do the job, they'll probably have access to someone who can. The FBI, maybe."

"All right." He caught the note of disappointment in her voice again.

"Are you going to Memphis to see Harriet's family now?" she asked.

"That's my plan."

"Have you looked outside? It's a five-hour trip, and now it's pouring rain."

A glance outside her window told him she was right. The sky had been overcast all day, as it often was at this time of year, but he hadn't noticed that the rain had begun. It was coming down in torrents and showing no signs of letting up.

"Then it'll be a five-hour trip back when your business is done. You'll be exhausted."

"I'll just have to be exhausted," he said. "My travel budget can't manage an overnight stay in Memphis."

"I have an alternate suggestion," she said, and she surprised herself when she said it. "Wait and go to Memphis in the morning. You'll be fresher, and you'll be able to make the entire trip in a day. In fact, I could go with you tomorrow; it might be easier to break the news to her family if I were along."

"My travel budget can't handle a hotel bill here, either," he said. "And I don't think my police jury would authorize an expenditure like that, especially so close to my office." The police jury was Louisiana's version of the county government.

"I have an alternative for that problem, too," she said. "You can stay here overnight. That way you don't have to return to your office. You can leave from here. Just tell your office that you stayed with a friend."

He turned away from her to stare again at the rain outside. It was, if anything, coming down harder than before. He could see rivulets streaming across the lawn of her apartment building and collecting in standing puddles in the low-lying areas. A steady stream poured off roof eaves and gushed from downspouts. Merely recrossing the Mississippi could be a risky endeavor, he told himself, though he was not certain he believed it.

Still, the apartment was comfortable, and the girl was attractive. It was an appealing offer.

"It's a very kind offer," he said, watching the rain. "But you realize that it would be a bit… snug for the two of us. I can sleep here on the sofa, but it would still be…"

He felt her arms slip tenderly around his waist, and then her hands turned his face toward hers.

"I like snug," she said. "Snug is nice."

NEW ORLEANS

OCTOBER 1812

"Are you out of your mind, sir?" said the lawyer.

"I do not believe so," said Henry Miller Shreve.

"The Fulton-Livingston firm has acquired a monopoly on steam boat transportation on the lower Mississippi River," said the lawyer, whose name was Duncan. "They acquired this monopoly from the Louisiana legislature, and they protect it diligently. Their agent here, Mr. Edward Livingston, gives no quarter."

"So I have heard," said Shreve.

"He will seek your ruination, regardless of your success or failure. If in fact you are successful, he will seize your boat. You cannot win under such circumstances."

"I disagree, sir. As for the seizure of my boat, I am counting on you to prevent it."

Lawyer Duncan sighed.

"Would that I could, sir. Your adversaries are quite wealthy, quite influential, and quite determined."

"I believe that it can be done."

"With the weight of the legislature behind them? Have you considered the expense of such an endeavor? The potential risk? You could lose everything you own."

"I understand my situation perfectly, and I believe I have an advantage that you have apparently not considered," Shreve said.

"And that is…"

"The Fulton-Levinson firm gained their monopoly by promising to establish steam-propelled commerce on the Mississippi. They convinced the legislature that they required a monopoly in order to justify the expense of their enterprise. If they are to maintain their monopoly, they must follow through on their promise."

"I understand they are quite close to achieving their objective."

Shreve laughed.

"They are nowhere near their objective," he said. "What is more, they will *never* achieve their goal as long as they continue barking up the wrong tree."

Duncan stood suddenly, inadvertently scattering a number of documents that had been cluttering his desk.

"Now hold, sir," he said with some heat. "You go too far, surely. Mr. Fulton, after all, *invented* the steam boat. Surely he can solve the relatively minor difficulties that remain!"

Shreve dismissed the lawyer's objections with a contemptuous wave.

"Mr. Fulton, sir, to my certain knowledge, has invented nothing," Shreve said, contemptuously. "He learned everything he knew from others—men who were far more capable than he, but who lacked Mr. Fulton's influential friends. He has left a trail of ruined careers in his wake. His great skill was the gift of sycophancy, which served him well but is no longer of any value."

"I have heard such," the lawyer admitted. "I was not certain whether to believe it."

"The inventor of the steamboat was a Mr. John Fitch of Connecticut," Shreve said. "Mr. Fitch was not a wealthy man, nor was he acquainted with men of wealth. Mr. Fulton, however, knew Mr. Livingston, and Mr. Livingston *was* a wealthy man."

"Nevertheless, Mr. Fulton's firm has the monopoly, and you do not," said Duncan. "What can you hope to do in the face of that?"

"The monopoly will exist only as long as no one succeeds in sailing upstream," Shreve replied. "The Fulton-Livingston firm has never sailed past Natchez, and they never will. Their vessels are fundamentally flawed."

"And you can succeed where they have failed?"

"I believe so," Shreve said.

Lawyer Duncan was silent for several minutes as he studied the man before him. He knew Henry Miller Shreve by name and reputation; New Orleans was not so large that a few prominent men could be lost in the mob. And Shreve had gained considerable prominence as one of the most successful keelboat men on the river.

Could what he was saying be possible? Was the monopoly actually as vulnerable as that? If someone could successfully negotiate the Mississippi with steam power—someone who was *not* a part of the monopoly—it would create tremendous pressure to open up the river to all. Merchants and traders all through the Mississippi valley and beyond, in Louisville and Little Rock, from Pittsburgh to Plaquemine, would be eager to take advantage of this opportunity. The legislature would be under considerable pressure to open the field to competition.

And the lawyer who made that happen would benefit from an enhanced reputation at the very least. It would not be wise to appear too eager, but…

"And there is another consideration that I have neglected to mention until now," said Shreve eventually.

"And that is…" Duncan prompted.

"We are at war," Shreve said. "New Orleans is—or will be—a prize in the war. The British will come for it, you may be sure."

"They are likely to get it," Duncan said, morosely. "New Orleans is a city of Creole gentlemen and free colored and, of course, slaves. The slaves cannot own guns, the freedmen are closely restricted, and the gentlemen are fit only for gambling, racing horses, and dueling. I suspect they will run away when the first shot is fired."

"Perhaps so," said Shreve. "But hundreds—even thousands—of men from the western states and territories are eager to join in the coming battle."

"Rubes," said Duncan. "Backwoods bumpkins who cannot even write their own names, most of them."

"But they *can* shoot, sir. Men who must make their own powder and shot learn quickly the virtue of accuracy. And New Orleans is the lifeblood of the western states and territories. Western men cannot afford to see New Orleans fall to the enemy, and they will come willingly to her defense."

"I hope you are right, sir."

"I am. They will come, and they will need a way to travel here in considerable numbers. If they could meet a steamboat in Natchez, say, that would bring them the rest of the way…"

"I see your point," said Duncan. "But fighting the monopoly will be an expensive proposition. I shall require considerable funds. Are you prepared to incur the expense that will be required?"

"I believe so. I have had several successful seasons on the river and have accumulated a considerable sum of capital, and I have backers, also."

"Well then, I believe we can do some business," Duncan said. "Would you care to join me in a glass? I have a quite agreeable Madeira here. I daresay you will not have tasted its like in Pennsylvania."

"I would be delighted," Shreve said.

So it was settled. Duncan smiled. Shreve smiled. And they drank the wine.

MEMPHIS, TENNESSEE

THE SIXTH DAY

A detective from the Memphis police department met Sprenkel in front of the Van Dorn residence.

It was a sprawling house, the sort of house known in the area as a "ranch" house, which always made Sprenkel think of horses and cattle. There were no horses or cattle in this neighborhood, although there were more than enough SUVs and pickup trucks to run a good-sized spread. There were also satellite dishes on nearly every rooftop and riding lawnmowers working industriously on several lawns. Even in this assemblage of affluence, the Van Dorn residence was distinguished by its size. Sprenkel hadn't been to Graceland, but he suspected Elvis Presley's mansion would suffer by comparison.

The detective, who introduced himself as Al Caulfield, led the way to the massive front door.

"I thought you said you were bringing the girl's roommate with you," Caulfield said.

"She had a conflict." Sprenkel shrugged.

Yesterday, Jill had begged to come with him when he broke the news to Harriet's family, but this morning her zeal had waned. She had been cool to him after last night. Sprenkel thought he understood her change of heart all too well.

"Probably just as well," Caulfield said. "That makes one less crying woman to have to deal with."

"Probably," Sprenkel said.

The house was closed tight. Sprenkel could hear a central air conditioning unit whining noisily somewhere.

"Maybe they can't hear you knocking."

"They ought to be able to hear the doorbell, though," Caulfield said. "Let's check around back. Maybe they got a swimming pool or a hot tub."

He led the way around the side of the house, and Sprenkel marveled at the size of the property. There had been places in the Maryland hunt country of a similar size, but there was nothing in Baltimore City to compare it with, he thought. Just circling the house seemed to take a very long time.

As Caulfield had predicted, there was a hot tub. Sprenkel wondered if it came as standard equipment with houses like this.

The tub was surrounded by a redwood stockade fence. They circled the fence until they reached the entrance.

"Shit," said Caulfield.

A nude woman sat in the tub, slumped over but upright. The water jets were silent, and the liquid was tinted with a slight pink stain.

"Shot in the head, looks like," Caulfield said.

"Probably not too long ago," Sprenkel added. "She's not all that cold yet."

"The water temperature could make it hard to tell for certain," Caulfield said. "If the tub was running when she died and the timer kept it running for a while afterward, it'll be a tough call to figure time of death."

"Not that long ago, though," Sprenkel said. "Matter of hours, not days."

"No maggots yet, I'd say," Caulfield added. "Hope you don't mind if I don't open her eyes to look for them."

"Your crime scene people can do that as well as we can."

"My thoughts, too," Caulfield said. "Guess I'd better call it in, though."

"One shot to the back of the head," Sprenkel said. "A gang execution? In Memphis?"

"Hey, we got half a million people here just in the city, not to mention the suburbs. We're a big city now. We got gangs just like any big city."

The crime scene investigators arrived speedily and began a thorough search of the house itself. There was another body inside, also shot through the back of the head. The third body, a young man in his twenties, was found sprawled near a door leading to the garage. His body was riddled with bullets; Sprenkel counted five entrance wounds in the young man's back.

"Probably trying to escape," said one of the investigators. "Looks like he almost made it."

"I need some air," Sprenkel said.

He walked cautiously to the front lawn, carefully avoiding the investigators, and sat in the shade of a massive red oak tree. Caulfield had said it had rained here yesterday, as it had in Natchez, but the ground here was already dry.

Caulfield joined him under the tree.

"I've been doing this for fifteen years or so, but it don't get any easier," he said.

"Twenty years for me."

"You were in Baltimore before, I heard. Why'd you come down here? Long way from home."

"That's why I came."

Caulfield considered that for a moment. He nodded.

"I can understand that," he said. "A change of scene can be good sometimes. Was it what you expected?"

"I didn't expect anything in particular. I just wanted to get away from there."

"Any particular reason?"

"It was a personal thing."

"All right. I don't need to know, I guess. I'm assuming you're not a fugitive, or anything."

"Not that I know of."

"Okay. You heading back to Louisiana now?"

"I've been away for a full day. Need to get back to the job, if I want to keep it."

"Right. I'll let you know what we find. Looks like we'll be here a while."

Sprenkel began the drive back to Louisiana. It was mid-day by now. The rain that had inundated the area during the previous day had mostly dried up in Memphis, but he saw increasing evidence of it as he drove south. As he drove through Mississippi he began to see puddles by the roadside.

He stopped at a roadside restaurant for coffee and was surprised to find that the ground was still soft. Returning to the car with his coffee, his shoes sank nearly an inch in the soft earth. And over the northern horizon, the rain clouds were forming again.

More rain was on the way. For some reason that he couldn't put his finger on, a sense of dread came over him. He remembered the lines from a Bob Dylan song:

"*Something is happening, and you don't know what it is*
"*Do you, Mr. Jones?*"

NEW ORLEANS

DECEMBER 1814

If someone had thought to ask him, Henry Miller Shreve would have admitted to feelings of trepidation as he approached New Orleans. As he steamed down the river and caught his first glimpse of the cathedral, there on the Place D'Armes, he sensed that a confrontation was imminent.

Although the *Enterprise* was the first steam-powered vessel under his command, Shreve had followed developments closely. There had been several attempts to establish steamboat transportation on the western rivers, but no one had yet succeeded. Nicholas Roosevelt had been the first man to successfully sail a steamboat *down* the Mississippi, but he had been unable to make the return trip. His boat was underpowered and could not cope with the strong downstream current. Roosevelt's boat spent its remaining days making the short jaunt from New Orleans to Natchez and back.

The lower Mississippi was a major obstacle, but Shreve thought it could be overcome. He believed that he was the man who would do so.

It would take the Livingston-Fulton company some time before they realized that another interloper was in their midst, but they *would* notice. Edward Livingston had spies everywhere, listening to gossip and barroom conversations, and—most certainly—watching the river for the approach of steam-powered vessels bent on usurping his monopoly rights.

Usurping the Fulton-Livingston monopoly was exactly what Shreve intended, and he thought he had a vessel worthy of the attempt. The *Enterprise* wasn't ideal—Shreve knew its weaknesses intimately—but it was closer to the ideal than anything that had plied the river up to now. It had been carrying passengers and cargo on the Ohio River between Brownsville, Pennsylvania and Louisville, Kentucky for six months, and it had made two successful upstream voyages against strong currents.

But a strong current on the Ohio River was not comparable to a strong current on the Mississippi. Shreve knew this better than most. He had taken command of the *Enterprise* from its previous captain in

December because the boat's owner knew of his intimate knowledge of the Mississippi, its vagaries and its pitfalls. If anyone could make the return voyage upstream from New Orleans, it was he. This was his chance.

"There's New Orleans now," said his pilot. "There's the church steeple."

Shreve, who had seen the spire of the cathedral several minutes earlier, simply acknowledged his pilot's remark. No instructions were necessary; the pilot knew what to do.

The boat began its laborious turn toward the riverbank, its giant rear paddlewheel thrashing fiercely, churning the brown-green water to a frothing fury as it crossed the powerful downstream current. The boat eased up to the levee, the crew secured it to the dock, and the great wheel grew silent. In the sudden stillness, Shreve could hear the creaking of the steam boiler, contracting as it cooled.

Now to business. His arrival had been anticipated; a letter of introduction had preceded him.

An escort now awaited him on the shore, a young army lieutenant sent by General Andrew Jackson. Shreve accompanied the soldier, resplendent in the spotless uniform expected of aides to a general officer, up Rue Royale, where Andrew Jackson awaited.

Shreve found Jackson in the front room of a row house that he had commandeered as his temporary headquarters. Jackson's orders were to protect New Orleans from the British, and he had moved quickly to shore up the city's inadequate defenses.

War with England was now more than two years old, and the United States had not fared well. Lately it had seen some successes, but the ultimate test would come in New Orleans. The city, which was the conduit for the young nation's international trade, was the key to America's survival. Americans knew this, and the British did, also.

The general was staring impatiently out at the street, where business seemed to have come to a standstill. He turned as Shreve entered. Shreve saw a tall, gaunt man whose massive head was crowned with hair that was already going to gray. Shreve estimated Jackson's age at about forty, although from a distance the hair would make him appear older.

"Captain Shreve, I presume?" Jackson's voice had the twang of the west, but Shreve thought he also heard the softer tones of the Carolina coast.

"I am, indeed, sir. Happy to make your acquaintance."

Jackson was not a man for pleasantries. He acknowledged the greeting with a curt nod and turned quickly to the business at hand.

"So what have you brought me in your infernal steam boat? Ammunition, I hope, and guns?"

"Indeed. Both ammunition *and* guns. Our hold is packed tight with them."

"Thank God!" Jackson said. "With your permission I'll send a regiment to the docks immediately to begin unloading. Our need is growing desperate."

"The unloading is already under way," Shreve said. "I gather that you expect an attack to be imminent."

"I don't know," Jackson said. "We must be prepared for it, in any event. And it cannot be very long, I'd think. They have already appeared at Mobile, and it is… what?… two or three weeks journey from here, at most."

"The British would move quickly, I should think," Shreve said.

"*Very* quickly. There's nothing the British like better than an uneven fight, one that is weighted in their favor, as they assume this to be."

"And is it in fact? Weighted in their favor?"

"I very much fear that it is, at present," Jackson said. "Your arms and ammunition will help, of course, if I can somehow procure sufficient men to use them."

"I will volunteer my services, General," Shreve said, surprising himself. He had been raised as a Quaker.

Jackson nodded.

"Thank you, Mr. Shreve. Your services might prove quite useful when the battle finally comes. For the moment, however, you are more important to me as a river boat captain. I expect to see men coming to the defense of New Orleans from all over the western states and territories. You could serve me best by meeting those men in Natchez, say, and ferrying them here. Can you do that?"

"Certainly," Shreve said. He paused, and then added: "There is one small matter, however, that you should be made aware of. My presence here violates a monopoly that was granted by the Louisiana legislature to the Livingston-Fulton company. If I do not leave the city soon, they will seize my vessel. They may, in fact, have done so already."

"I have heard about the monopoly," Jackson said. "Did you not take this into account before you came downriver?"

"I did, sir. I have obtained legal counsel to fight them, if it becomes necessary."

"And your chances of success?"

"Good, I think. Mr. Fulton's boats have been unable to sail successfully against the current of the river. If I can do so—as I believe I can—the company will have a difficult time maintaining their monopoly in the face of popular demand."

"Well, time is of the essence," Jackson said. "As the man responsible for the defense of the city, I can temporarily supersede the legislature. You'll have no problems with the monopolists as long as the British threaten New Orleans."

"And afterward?"

Jackson favored him with a grim smile.

"Afterward, Mr. Shreve, I'd advise you to run like hell."

"Exactly what I had in mind, sir," Shreve said.

* * * *

The *Enterprise* made several trips to Natchez, bringing boatloads of frontiersmen with their trusted rifles to the city of New Orleans and returning for yet another complement of men. In the hold the crew also packed food and other provisions for the city's survival during the coming troubles.

The British advanced cautiously from the east through bayous and estuaries, rather than up the Mississippi. Although the Americans lost five gunboats that had been stationed on the river to protect the city, they held off the advance and suffered few casualties.

The British struck two days before Christmas in an attempt to establish a foothold among the plantations south of the city. It was a bloody battle with hundreds of casualties on both sides, but it ended inconclusively. A second attack followed on New Year's Day, again producing casualties on both sides.

For the next week, the British concentrated on strengthening their position by moving artillery in place and bringing in reinforcements. Early on the morning of January 8, they struck in force.

The battle, when it finally occurred, was something of an anticlimax. It was over in little more than half an hour, and the outcome was clear. The British lost more than 2,000 men, thanks in large measure to the marksmanship of Jackson's backwoods volunteers, whose experience with their rifles overpowered the British numerical superiority. The Americans killed two British generals and severely wounded a third, forcing their retreat back the way they had come. Jackson lost 71 men.

Shreve joined the forces on the ramparts. Whatever misgivings he might have had about violating his Quaker principles, they seemed to vanish in the current circumstances.

The British were vanquished. The Americans were astonished and giddy with excitement. The armies that had defeated the great Napoleon had been crushed by a small band of Frenchmen and backwoodsmen. It was an eventuality that no one, on either side, had anticipated.

Shreve hurried back from the battlefield, but he returned too late. As he approached the docks he saw several armed men standing around the *Enterprise*.

As he stared forlornly at the scene before him, a familiar figure appeared on the deck. They had never met, but Shreve knew him, had seen him around the town, and had heard all the stories from other river men. Edward Livingston had wasted no time in confiscating the *Enterprise*.

Rather than continue on down to his boat, Shreve turned on his heel and strode away toward the town. Another battle now loomed—a battle not of guns, but of lawyers.

CONCORDIA PARISH

THE SEVENTH DAY

"I don't know what the odds of this are," said Levesque, "but we got a match on that DNA."

"What DNA?"

"The DNA we found in the cunt of the dead girl out by Old River. Turns out it matches a stiff that turned up in the French Quarter a couple of days ago. Name of Angelo Sweet."

Sprenkel thought about that. "New Orleans is near two-hundred miles from here. How'd he get down there, I wonder?"

"Well, he didn't walk," said Levesque. "And the river might carry him down there, depending on where he went in, but it couldn't pick him up out of the water and deposit him on a downtown street corner."

"Have they done the autopsy yet?"

"Not yet."

"I think," said Sprenkel, "that we need to take a look at that body"

They left the next day. Sprenkel sat in the front passenger seat of the cruiser and stared, mesmerized, at the expanse of water to his right. The bayous were dotted with cypress trees, their limbs laden with Spanish moss and their roots poking above the surface of the water. The locals called these roots "knees," and the similarity was unmistakable. They reminded Sprenkel of a woman lying in bed, waiting to receive a lover.

Levesque was driving. Generally, Sprenkel liked to drive, but he wasn't familiar enough with New Orleans to chance it on his own.

"Too bad we can't stay overnight," Levesque said. "New Orleans is a great nighttime city."

"We can't."

"Oh, I know that. It's just a shame, is all I'm sayin'. I could show you places you couldn't even imagine."

"This is no pleasure trip," Sprenkel said.

"You got that right," said Levesque. "Still, there's no reason not to have a little fun while we're there."

"I'll take it under advisement," Sprenkel said.

The road south followed the levees. Sprenkel always marveled at the ways in which everyday living here was determined by the river. People fished in lakes that existed only because the river had changed course and cut off a river bend, sealing it off from the main current. The river wandered continually and confusingly, making talk of directionality absurd and meaningless. In New Orleans, he had been told, the west bank of the river was actually east of the city much of the time, and, consequently, the sun rose in New Orleans over the west bank and set over the east. Sprenkel found it confusing, even after six years living here.

They entered the city from the west—or was it the east?—and crossed the ubiquitous river yet again.

"So we're downtown now?" Sprenkel asked, seeing the city skyline to their right.

"No. We're uptown."

"There's a difference?"

"Sure. Downtown's to our right. This is uptown."

"Oh."

"Based on the river," Levesque said. "Uptown is upstream. Downtown is downstream."

"Why don't they just say that?"

"What?"

"Upstream and downstream. Why not say that? Why uptown and downtown?"

"Beats me. Guess it's a Creole thing."

"A what?"

"Never mind. It'd take too long."

"I've been hearing that a lot since I got to Louisiana," Sprenkel said.

"Well, we do some things different down here."

At the morgue they met with an assistant medical examiner and a female detective from the Eighth District on Royal Street. The AME, whose name was Dawkins, offered coffee, which Sprenkel declined and Levesque accepted eagerly. The detective, Sprenkel noted, also declined the offer.

As the examiner poured coffee from an electric coffee maker, Sprenkel studied his companions. The detective was, he thought, somewhere in her forties—probably closer to fifty—but well preserved for all that. There was gray sprinkled among the dark hair, which she wore short, in a style that might equally have suited a man, if he were a leading man in the movies. Her name, she said, was Graziano.

"What's your first name?" Sprenkel asked.

"Sergeant," she said.

Dawkins had the pale complexion and the bottom-heavy shape of a man who spent most of his life indoors. Sprenkel thought he was remarkably cheerful for a man who specialized in corpses.

"All right," said Dawkins after distributing coffees. "You're interested in which case, now?"

Sprenkel told him.

"Ah, yes, the shooting in the Quarter." He picked up a manila file folder and began leafing through its contents. "Not much to tell, really. It was fairly straightforward. Shot twice in the back of the head. Death was instantaneous, or as near to it as makes no difference."

"Where was he shot?"

"I just told you. Back of the head."

"I meant," Sprenkel said, "was he shot where he was found?"

"Oh. No, he wasn't. I can't tell you where he *was* shot, of course, but it wasn't where he was found. He was moved post-mortem."

"How long had he been dead when he was found?"

"Well, now," Dawkins said. "Time of death is hard to pin down; it involves a lot of guesswork. Based on body temperature and the lack of rigor, I'd say about six hours. Ambient temperature can affect decomposition, you know, and it's been pretty warm lately."

"So it might have been later."

"Maybe."

"And he was found…"

Dawkins consulted his notes. "About six in the morning, looks like." He glanced at Graziano. "That sound about right to you?"

"About that, yes," she replied.

"So he was shot sometime around midnight and moved to the Quarter from somewhere else," Sprenkel said. "Do you have a name for this guy?"

Dawkins consulted his notes again.

"He had a driver's license that said he was Angelo Sweet, home address in Shreveport. They're checking next-of-kin now."

Sprenkel turned to the detective.

"Got any theories about this?" he asked.

Graziano shrugged. "I try to let the facts guide me, Sheriff. So far I don't have much. We know he was moved to where we found him, but we don't know from where."

"Had he been in the river?"

Graziano looked to Dawkins.

"Not as far as we can tell," Dawkins said. "And I think we'd be able to tell."

"Tell me, Sheriff," said Graziano. "What's your interest in this? It's a New Orleans crime."

"This guy's semen turned up in a dead hooker we found up on a levee on our turf," Sprenkel said. "I'm trying to make the connections. The fact that he and the hooker were killed so far apart is interesting."

"Might not necessarily mean anything," said the detective.

"True enough," said Sprenkel. "But I'd like to know."

The detective nodded. "I'll look into it. Anything else?"

"Any hookers go missing recently?" Sprenkel asked. "We've got one we can't seem to account for. She went by Madeleine… d'Anjou."

"I'll ask around," said the detective. "We don't exactly take a census of prostitutes."

* * * *

Levesque took Sprenkel's decision not to remain in New Orleans with good grace. They switched off driving on the way back, stopping for dinner—Levesque called it "supper"—on the way, and arrived at the office shortly before midnight. Levesque went home to his family. Sprenkel returned to his office. Eventually he fell asleep at his desk.

CONCORDIA PARISH

THE NINTH DAY

"I never knew how many airfields we have around here," Levesque said. He laid a sheaf of papers on Sprenkel's desk, the fruits of a couple of days spent in online searches.

"How many *are* there?" Sprenkel said. "And what do you mean by 'around here?'"

"I'm just looking at Louisiana and Mississippi so far," Levesque said. "And I count… I don't know… thirty or forty. And that don't count the *real* airports, like Baton Rouge or Jackson. Some of these are just flat stretches of cow pasture, but if they're big enough, somebody probably has landed a plane on them."

"Around here," Sprenkel said, dryly, "*all* the pastures are flat." A quick glance out of the window confirmed his observation and reminded him that he would much prefer to be outside on this, the first day of unalloyed sunshine in a week.

"You got that right," Levesque said. "And I haven't even started to look at the *abandoned* airfields. There's probably a dozen or so of those."

For a moment, Sprenkel had to wrench himself back to the present. "Abandoned? Who abandons an airport?"

"The Feds, mostly," Levesque said. "They're old air bases, or World War II training bases, or maintenance facilities. The government gives them up, figuring they don't need them anymore. So the fields just sit there vacant, because nobody else wants them either."

"Penny-wise and pound-foolish," Sprenkel said.

"Well, hell," Levesque said. "Penny-wise and pound-foolish—that's official government policy."

"You got a map of these abandoned airfields?" Sprenkel said.

Levesque pulled out a map from a drawer in his desk and spread it out. Sprenkel came and looked over his shoulder.

"Where'd you get this?"

"Off the internet," Levesque said. "You can get just about anything on the internet."

Sprenkel pointed to a spot on the map. "This one looks just about perfect," he said. "About the right distance from us. Maybe halfway between Memphis and Natchez. You think somebody could fly in and out of there without causing a stir in the town here? The base is abandoned, after all."

"So is the town, I suspect," Levesque said. "A lot of these little towns only hung on because of the federal government. If you close up the base, you might as well roll up the town at the same time. Planes could probably fly in and out of there every day, and nobody'd ever be around to notice."

"Don't they have to file a flight plan or something?"

"If you leave from nowhere and fly to another nowhere, who's gonna know?"

Sprenkel stared at the map a moment longer, but he had already made a decision.

"I think we'd better go check this one out ourselves," he said.

RURAL MISSISSIPPI

THE NINTH DAY

"This doesn't look too promising," Sprenkel said.

"Sure doesn't," Levesque said. "Don't think this road's been used much in the past few years."

"Well, we're here now," Sprenkel said. "We might as well follow it, see where it goes."

"It's too narrow to turn around right here, anyway."

The road was, indeed, narrow—barely more than a car's width—with steep drainage ditches on either side. It had been paved at one time, but there wasn't much pavement left. Aside from teenage beer busts and make-out parties, Sprenkel doubted that anyone came this way by choice any more.

The road wound through tall grass and cattails so high that a small man might have difficulty seeing over the growth. The dust kicked up by a vehicle, such as the Ford Crown Vic they were riding in now, would further complicate visibility.

Of course, an aircraft wouldn't have that problem, he thought. Not if it had a paved runway.

"I think maybe we're here," Levesque said. "Looks like a landing strip up there to our left."

It wasn't much of a landing strip. There was only one runway, as far as Sprenkel could see. It was no more than five-hundred feet in length and barely twenty feet wide. In addition to the runway, there was a small clapboard building, which could have housed either an office or tools. An ancient gasoline pump of the type used in the forties stood forlornly beside the shack.

"I don't think this is the place," Levesque said. "Look at that runway. Potholes the size of bomb craters. This place hasn't been used for aircraft for a long time."

"I think you're right," Sprenkel said. "But we'd better check more carefully, just to make certain. We've come all this way."

"I've got the camera with me. I'll go get some shots of the runway while we're here."

"While you do that, I'll check out this… terminal building," Sprenkel said. "Maybe somebody left a clue or two behind."

"Like a signed confession, or something," Levesque said. "Right. Maybe I'll get lucky and find something out on the runway. A bloody handkerchief, maybe, with the vic's DNA on it and the perp's fingerprints."

The building, apparently, had been both an office and a tool shed. An old steel desk stood in the center of the single room, and an ancient typewriter sat forlornly on the extension. A broken-handled shovel still rested against a corner wall, although Sprenkel suspected that it had once had companions, long-since removed.

He found no bloody handkerchiefs. There were mouse droppings in abundance, however, there were several cigarette butts, including some that had been hand-rolled and had, Sprenkel suspected, contained marijuana. Sprenkel wasn't particularly interested in them; he had enough on his plate at the moment without pursuing teenage potheads who might not even live in the area and who were, moreover, outside his jurisdiction. There was nothing else of interest, as far as he could ascertain.

But as he turned to leave, something caught his eye: a bit of red candle wax on the surface of the desk. He could tell that it had been a candle because, although there was not much left, a bit of wick still protruded.

There was only one, and it could have an innocent explanation. The shack had been wired for electricity, but the power had been turned off—probably for a long time. He checked the fuse box. The fuses were still good, as far as he could determine, but no juice was passing through them. The power had probably been turned off at a central location, standard procedure for a building that no one intended to be using.

So why the candle? Perhaps it set the mood for an evening of teenage sex. Or it served as a cigarette lighter for a pot-smoking party. Whatever the case, it wasn't worth pursuing at the moment. He had bigger problems.

Levesque was returning from his photographic inspection of the runway. Reluctantly, because he was troubled by a disquieting feeling that he had missed something, Sprenkel returned to his office across the river.

* * * *

Someone was waiting for him before he could step inside the station. "Sheriff Sprenkel."

Not a question, precisely; more a statement of fact that the speaker was challenging Sprenkel to dispute. Sprenkel turned from the station door to see a man in his late thirties perhaps, thinning light brown hair topping a pleasant-looking face. He looked up at Sprenkel from behind the wheel of a recent-model Ford Mustang, now idling at the entrance of the parking area.

"I'm Sprenkel."

The man smiled and got out of the car.

"Harry Eastwood," the man said, extending his hand. "I've been hoping to meet you. I've been by your office a couple of times, but you weren't in."

"Do you live in the parish, Mr. Eastwood? I don't believe I've heard your name before, and it's a small parish."

"I'm new to the area," Eastwood said. "Only been here about a month. I live over in Ferriday."

"So what can I do for you, sir?"

"Well," Eastwood began. "This is a little irregular, but I'm looking for a good fishing spot. I figured that you would get around in the county—sorry, parish—and might have some ideas about that."

"I don't fish," Sprenkel said. "Don't have time, I'm afraid. But I don't think you'll have much trouble in that line. If there's one thing Louisiana is good for, it's fishing. There's water just about everywhere, as you may have noticed."

"I've noticed," Eastwood said. "I thought you might have found a favorite spot or two. Sorry to have bothered you."

"No bother, sir. Good luck to you."

As Eastwood walked away, Levesque appeared at Sprenkel's side.

"Who's he?" Levesque asked.

"Says his name is Eastwood," Sprenkel said. "Says he's new, lives in Ferriday. Ever see him before?"

"No."

"It might be useful to check him out," Sprenkel said. "White man living in Ferriday is a little strange, seems to me. Ferriday's... what... ninety percent black?"

"Something like that. Not ninety percent, but pretty high. Of course, this *is* the New South, you know."

"It's not that new."

"You're right about that," Levesque said. "I'll see what I can turn up. I'd probably look him up on my own, anyway. On account of his bumper sticker."

"I didn't notice."

"It said: 'Violence is an affront to God,'" Levesque said. "I've always thought God sorta got off on it."

THE MISSISSIPPI RIVER

THE NINTH DAY

The Man of God stood on the river bank and studied the concrete structure, silently calculating formulas and strategies. The current was deceptive, but he could see a swirling eddy that indicated the existence of scouring on the river bed at the base of the structure. That would be the place to act, he thought; where he could add his bit of encouragement to nature's own plans.

God's plans.

He was not one of those fundamentalists who believed that the world had been created in seven days out of nothing, in exactly the form in which it existed today. He knew the planet had undergone many changes and had seen many creatures that roamed the earth no more. He had seen the skeletons in the museum in Chicago: hulking creatures unlike anything that walked the earth today. He had nothing but contempt for those who insisted that evolution had not been proved. They were not merely wrong, but wrongheaded.

Whether it had happened over millions of years, as the evolutionists claimed, or only thousands, as the biblical fundamentalists claimed, was not important. The important thing was that the world had changed—the *river* had changed—and would change again.

The river was constantly probing. People tended to forget that. Even the engineers—the men who had built this structure—should know better. They were merely buying time. Humans could only delay the inevitable.

As it was, the river was kept at bay only by prodigious effort. The Man of God was looking at the symbol of those efforts: the Army Corps of Engineers called it the Old River Control Structure. The structure performed this function by regulating the amount of water permitted to enter the Atchafalaya—the steeper, shorter course to the Gulf. In normal conditions, about a third of the Mississippi's water was permitted to enter the Atchafalaya. In flood conditions, a greater amount of water was let through. It was all carefully calculated to prevent the Mississippi from responding to the forces of nature and, in essence, *becoming* the Atchafalaya, while also diverting enough water to protect the Atchafalaya wetlands. If the river were to take over the Atchafalaya, New Orleans and Baton Rouge would be doomed. The Mississippi south of Baton Rouge would be reduced to a tidal estuary. The mighty river would become a bayou dotted with mud flats and sand bars. The harbor would cease to exist. Deprived of their source of drinking water, the city itself, for all practical purposes, would die.

And good riddance to it. To many people, enthralled by the tawdry glamor of the city they called the Big Easy, such an event would be disastrous. To the Man of God, it seemed only just. An insidious evil would be wiped away, and a righteous new era would begin. Sodom would be destroyed, and he would be the instrument of its destruction.

He was not normally an excitable man, but this vision of the future pleased him immensely, and it filled him with pride to think that he would have a hand in it. He permitted himself a brief smile before he returned to his work.

The rain had picked up, and he hurried back to his truck. Not long now, he thought. Not long at all.

ENROUTE TO NEW YORK

THE TENTH DAY

The Man of God had a distasteful task to perform, but no one else could do it. It required that he go to New York City, a city he detested.

From his train window, he stared morosely at the ticky-tack houses and ramshackle, mostly derelict, factory buildings. The Acela express train, Amtrak's proud new weapon in the war for the loyalty of the impatient and well-heeled business traveler, was slowing as it approached the station in downtown Newark.

Dawn had broken an hour or so earlier, but it was difficult to tell in the gray haze of the urban landscape. The accumulated grime of decades of coal-burning and automobile exhaust fumes had turned the city—indeed the entire Eastern Seaboard—into a depressing, featureless jumble of brick and mortar, asphalt, and dirt.

It was fashionable to speak of God's creation, but this… dog's breakfast… was not God's doing. This was, manifestly, the work of Man, for which he would someday be called to account. The Man of God had few certainties in his belief system, but this was one of them. There would be a Day of Judgment, and the judgment would be swift and certain. And painful.

In the meantime, it was the responsibility of those men and women who could see the truth to do what needed to be done. The Man of God knew his duty.

His journey had begun in Washington, DC, where he was given the necessary instructions. There he was told that he would need to go to New York.

He was doing so now.

The train had arrived in Newark and was now sitting quietly in the gloom of the station. The Man of God sat looking out at the dark platform. A crowd of men and women had been standing there when the train had pulled in, but the throng had quickly disappeared with no apparent trace. The train seemed to have swallowed them up.

And now they were leaving Newark. A few passengers straggled into the car, fighting the movement of the train and balancing briefcases and computer bags as they searched for an open seat. There were plenty of seats available; the car was less than half full, but the new passengers treated the search for a place to sit with the gravity usually reserved for matters of national security.

The Man of God watched as the neat young men and the smartly dressed women passed by, and he marveled at the grim determination on their faces. The sheer futility of their exertions, and the disenchantment that inevitably awaited them, caused a momentary sensation of empathy. They were so unwavering in their pursuit of a goal that would inexorably leave them disillusioned and bereft of much of the joy of living.

I've been there, the Man of God thought. *I should tell them. They deserve to know that they're chasing a will-o-the-wisp.*

But he knew already that the effort would be fruitless. Some might listen to him, but none would hear. They would have to learn on their own. He promised himself, again, that he would do what he could to help them learn.

He sighed and leaned back in his seat. The train was moving again, and New York was the next stop.

The Man of God rarely came to New York, any more. At one time he had been a regular visitor—his business had required it—but he had never learned his way around Penn Station. Every time he came to the city he would lose his way in the labyrinthine railroad station and spent long minutes finding his way out.

This day was no exception. For nearly an hour he wandered through the teeming lobby, looking for the signs that would lead him up to street level. There was no shortage of signs, actually, but the signs seemed to contradict themselves. He would set off in the direction that seemed to be indicated by an arrow on an overhead sign, only to discover that he was not, in the end, where he had expected to be.

He muttered under his breath. He was tempted to curse, but his principles would not permit it.

Eventually, all other options having been tried, he found his way to the surface. He stood on the street corner in the gray morning light and considered his next move. His ultimate destination was uptown and easily accessible to the subway, but he had had enough of subterranean places. Although he begrudged the expense, he decided to hire a cab.

The driver who picked him up wore a turban, which gave the Man of God a moment's pause. He decided after a brief hesitation that the man was not Muslim, but Sikh. He would be safe with this man, he concluded.

"Where to?" the driver asked. He had an accent that the Man of God could not place. Not Indian or Pakistani, at least not purely. Something else. Something the Man of God found vaguely familiar.

"North," the Man of God said.

"Think you could narrow it down a little more? There's an awful lot of north out there."

"Just head north," the Man of God said. "I'll direct you when we get closer."

"Oh, good," the driver said. "I love an adventure. Any particular route you want me to take?"

"Riverside Drive," said the Man of God.

"You got it."

Of course, the Man of God thought to himself. *Brooklyn!* The man might be South Asian in origin, but he had spent much of his life right here. It was interesting that his accent sounded so much like South Louisiana.

Like New Orleans, in fact. Would he *never* be rid of that sound?

NATCHEZ, MISSISSIPPI

THE TENTH DAY

Search engines, thought Jill Winston. Why hadn't I thought of them before?

Like most graduate students, she was adept at pursuing information on the internet, but somehow the idea of using it for this particular search had not previously dawned on her.

When she had first learned of the murder, she had spent many hours wondering and worrying about Harriet's sad fate. Her attempts to find an explanation had been fruitless, and she realized eventually that she really knew very little about her roommate. Despite having lived together for two years, their acquaintance had been remote, even a bit formal. They seldom talked, especially about personal matters, and in recent months had seldom even seen each other except in passing.

Now, she was startled to find, Harriet had not been in class—or even enrolled—for an entire academic year. She had left the apartment each morning, and Jill had assumed that she was on her way to class. What had she been doing with herself all that time?

Well, actually, what she had been doing had apparently been established, and it was both unsavory and illegal. Jill had difficulty reconciling the Harriet she had known with the image of the French Quarter prostitute that had been painted of her by the police and by that sheriff across the river. Harriet was not a prude—there had been men in her life, and sex as well—but she was conservative to a fault. The Harriet whom Jill knew—or thought she knew—would never have dressed like a harlot in what Harriet had once described contemptuously as "strumpet chic."

Clearly, there was more to Harriet than had been apparent to those around her. Jill wondered if her family had known about her roommate's avocation. She had met Harriet's mother only once, but she did not strike her as likely to forgive behavior as unseemly as that. She had no idea about Harriet's father, whom she had not met.

She concluded, with some chagrin, that she knew virtually nothing about her roommate and even less about her family. It was a defect that she wanted to remedy, but she blundered around for some time with no real sense of how to go about it.

It was then that search engines came to mind. She knew some people used them to look up old friends, former lovers, and long-lost relatives. Maybe she could learn more about Harriet's past through the internet.

She logged on and tried a couple, not really expecting to find anything of interest. Surprisingly, Harriet's name turned up twice. One entry was from a newspaper, listing the names of high school graduates who were members of the National Honor Society. The other entry was from the university, announcing the names of students who had achieved honors at graduation.

There was one curious note, Jill thought. The university announcement noted that Harriet's home address was in Memphis. The earlier story, about her high school honors, came from a newspaper in Morgan City, Louisiana.

Morgan City. Where was Morgan City? Jill had heard the name before, but it was merely a place name to her. She launched a search for Morgan City, and the web site of the chamber of commerce appeared. Morgan City was a relatively small city in southern Louisiana, near the mouth of a river with a strange name. The name of the river appeared to be an amalgam of French and American Indian and who knew what else.

She tried sounding it out: At-CHAF-a-lie-yah. She was certain that she had never heard a name like that before, and yet the river appeared on the map to be quite large. It spread out, of course, as it approached the Gulf of Mexico, but even upstream it was broad and, she suspected, deep enough for ship traffic. A miniature Mississippi.

She found aerial and satellite photos of the city, which made it clear that Morgan City was dedicated to oil. Oil rigs, storage tanks, and tanker ships were everywhere.

Hadn't Harriet said something about oil once? Her father was an oil man? That might have been it. What was his name? She thought she had heard it once, but she couldn't remember it. Was it Robert? Ronald? Rodney? The name eluded her.

In frustration, she tried various combinations of the information she had: Van Dorn, oil, Morgan City, Harriet, Memphis. When one search engine failed to turn up anything of interest, she tried another. And another. There were so many from which to choose and so many possible combinations.

Her persistence astonished—and frightened—her. She had no official role in the investigation of Harriet's murder and, it could be argued, no business conducting an investigation on her own. She knew all this, and yet she continued to search. She told herself that her dissertation was on track to be completed on time, so she could spare the time to do some research on Harriet. But in her heart she knew the real reason she continued the exploration.

It was him. Sprenkel.

She had been attracted to him, and he had rejected her. She had never before made overtures to another man, or needed to, and Sprenkel's rejection stung deeply. Rationally, she knew there could be a hundred reasons for his rejection, most of which would not reflect on her. Indeed, he had emphasized that point in turning her down. But reason had nothing to do with it. The rejection, however gentle, still rankled.

It wasn't that he was devastatingly handsome. With his blond—almost white—hair and fair complexion, he looked a bit like a kewpie doll, not her idea of masculine magnificence. She had always preferred men with hairy chests, and she suspected Sprenkel's chest was as bare as a baby's. But something about him stuck in her mind, in spite of it all. Perhaps it was that gesture of spreading his coat for her on the rain-wet park bench that day on the college campus. It was silly, but it had stayed with her.

And she did want to know why Harriet had been so cruelly treated, and to know that whoever had murdered her would be brought to some sort of justice. Jill couldn't help with the police investigation—such as it was—but she might, by nibbling around the edges, discover some tidbit of information that could prove useful. It was worth a try.

So it was back to the search engines. With a heavy sigh, she returned to her keyboard.

THE MISSISSIPPI RIVER

APRIL 1815

Somewhere above Natchez, the troubles began. The *Enterprise* began to lose its battle with the river.

It began as softly as a whisper. Shreve was out of the pilot house, in his makeshift office working on his accounts, when he felt rather than heard the engine laboring. He tried to ignore it at first, but the vibrations grew stronger and more strained. The trembling was soon accompanied by a deep rumble, still more felt than heard, which told him that the engine had nearly reached its limits.

He rushed from his office, fearing the worst. A glance at the pressure gauge confirmed what his ear—and his gut—had told him. The engine was at the brink of collapse.

The engine was the largest ever built for a riverboat, and yet it was, apparently, still inadequate. Earlier in the year perhaps, before the spring thaws up north had engulfed the riverbed, it might have endured, but Shreve had been unable to leave sooner. In January he had been engaged with a cannon, fighting the British.

In the pilot house, consternation reigned.

"She's tryin' hard, captain," the wheelman said. "She just ain't strong enough. We're gonna have to pull over and tie up. Unless you got some better idea."

"Let me think a minute," Shreve said.

There would be no point in putting in to shore, not unless they were prepared to remain there for weeks, and perhaps for months. The spring floods were among them, and it could be a long delay until the boat would be able to hold its own. He could not afford to pay his crew for a month or more of enforced idleness.

If the *Enterprise* were a keelboat, she could be wrestled upstream by brute force. But the Enterprise was far too large to be moved by human power. If he could not move the boat by steam, he would be forced to admit defeat. The humiliation would be hard to endure, not to mention the harm it would cause to his future hopes. Would any investor be willing to commit to his next endeavor, after this?

In frustration, Shreve paced the deck and wracked his mind for a solution to his problem. The *Enterprise* was still making headway, but she was slowing dramatically. It was only a matter of time before her forward momentum halted, and she began to slip back downstream.

On both banks, meanwhile, Shreve could see river water pouring through crevasses in the levees. Not unconscious to the irony of his situation, he noted that some of the crevasses were wide enough to accommodate a boat the size of the *Enterprise*. And a further irony: considering the volume of water gushing through the crevasses, there was probably…

Enough water to float a boat!

The enormity of the situation, and the audacity of the solution that suddenly struck his fancy, made him laugh out loud.

"Quick-like, make for that crevasse!" he told his helmsman. The man looked at him incredulously, but something in Shreve's eye made him stifle his response. Instead, he wrenched the wheel sharply to the right. The boat, no longer fighting the current head-on, lurched forward for a moment and then began inching its way across the channel. As it approached the crevasse, the helmsman looked questioningly at Shreve.

"Don't dawdle! We haven't time!" Shreve shouted.

The boat plunged ahead and passed through the crevasse with relative ease. On the other side, Shreve was greeted by standing water.

It was not actually standing water, he realized, but there was no longer the furious downstream current with which to contend. And the water was deep enough to accommodate the *Enterprise*. Rather than fighting the river, the boat could sail in relative calm through the flooded cotton fields!

Shreve smiled. "Full steam ahead," he told the helmsman.

Sooner or later he might have to find another crevasse, in order to return to the river channel. Or maybe not, if the Ohio River also had flooded its banks. When the time came to return to the river, perhaps it would be the relatively more placid Ohio that they rejoined.

He allowed himself a moment of satisfaction before making a mental note to himself: his next boat—his boat—would have a more powerful engine, and he would have *two* of them.

SHREVEPORT, LOUISIANA

THE ELEVENTH DAY

"Kind of a quiet town, seems like," Sprenkel said to his deputy. "Third largest town in the state, did you say?"

"After New Orleans and Baton Rouge," Levesque confirmed. "Or maybe Baton Rouge is first, now, and New Orleans is second. Lot of people left New Orleans after Katrina."

"I guess I expected a little more action from a town this size. Doesn't seem like a town with a quarter-million people," Sprenkel said.

"And that's just Shreveport," Levesque said. "There's another sixty-thousand or so people across the river in Bossier City. Matter of fact, that's really where the action is. Most of the casinos are across the river."

"Then I guess we better check over there, too," Sprenkel said. "We're sure coming up dry on this side of the river."

The trip to Shreveport had taken more than three hours, so it was late morning before they arrived. It did not take very long to ascertain that no one named Angelo Sweet appeared on either the tax lists or voter registration rolls. A quick check across the river was no more fruitful.

Sprenkel was dreading the return trip. Fortunately, he was on his own time, so there should be no repercussions from his superiors. Levesque was on the parish's clock, but Sprenkel would vouch for him. He was certain that Levesque would not consider this a pleasure trip.

"You know where we should be looking?" Levesque said, breaking into Sprenkel's thoughts. "What was the address on that driver's license? We ought to go look at the place where he told the state he was living."

"You're right. I should have thought of that," Sprenkel said. "My skills are slipping. Maybe it's Alzheimer's or something."

"Maybe it's because you got too much on your mind."

"Or maybe it's heat stroke."

"In April?"

"Whatever," Sprenkel said. "Start the car."

They knew long before they reached the address that it was bogus. The search took them to a section of the city dominated by warehouses, most of which looked to be occupied—although not for residential purposes. Finally, they found the address that "Angelo Sweet" had listed on his driver's license.

They found a vacant corner lot, grown up in weeds and honeysuckle.

"Shit," Sprenkel said.

"I don't know," Levesque said. "The weeds are pretty high. I could poke around in there, maybe find a refrigerator carton that he called home."

"Sure," said Sprenkel. "Go ahead, but check for chiggers before you get back in the car."

Levesque continued to sit behind the wheel.

"Nah," he said, finally. "On second thought, with all the rain we've had, a refrigerator carton would have fallen apart by now."

"Yeah."

"So," said Levesque. "Can we go home now?"

"Might as well."

Levesque switched on the ignition. As he pulled away from the curb, he said, "You know it's going to be real late when we get home. Do I get to take some comp time tomorrow to make up for it?"

"Sure," said Sprenkel. "Sleep in tomorrow. I won't need you until… oh… almost nine o'clock."

MORGAN CITY, LOUISIANA

THE ELEVENTH DAY

Morgan City, Jill concluded, was not a place to write home about, not that she had planned to do so. It was a smallish city, flat like most everything in Louisiana, with a Cajun flavor and a seemingly all-consuming concern with oil.

In the ten-years-old city directory, which she found at the local library, she found a listing for a Roger Van Dorn, oil exploration engineer, with an address in a rather decrepit downtown office building. She decided to check it out.

There was no Roger Van Dorn on the wall directory, but she hadn't expected to find it there after so many years. Evidently the family had moved to Memphis some time ago. Still, she made the rounds, stopping in at every office in the building, and inquiring about Van Dorn. None of the tenants had been there long enough to remember him.

Except one.

He was a frail-looking man, probably in his eighties, with a shock of white hair that fell in his eyes when he laughed. He wore a blue, oxford cloth button-down dress shirt, with a button missing down near his beltline, and a striped necktie in Princeton University colors. He chain-smoked cigarettes. Jill thought he might be close to death, probably from lung cancer.

The man said he was a lawyer himself, and that Van Dorn had occupied the office adjacent to his. They had not been close; Van Dorn had had an annoying habit of shouting angrily into the phone whenever he encountered difficulties. He waved his cigarette as he spoke.

"What did he yell about?" Jill said, repressing her urge to cough violently from the smoke.

"Can't tell you that. I never did understand that stuff. Sounded like real estate talk, mostly. Can't even guarantee that, though."

"What *sorts* of things did he say?"

"Well, let me think on it a minute," he said. He made a great show of cogitating, during which an impressive clump of ash teetered on the end of his cigarette, dropped off, and plunged precipitously into the blue broadcloth abyss.

"You know," he said after a moment, "he talked about map coordinates, seems like. And maybe fence lines. He'd say things like 'two-hundred rods,' or 'six chains.' That's what made me think of real estate. A lot of old deeds measure land in terms of rods and chains."

"If he was supervising oil exploration, wouldn't he be using those same terms?" Jill asked.

"Depends," said the lawyer. "Maybe, if he was looking for underground oil deposits. But there's not much land exploration going on around here. Offshore, now, there's more of it."

"If he were exploring offshore," Jill said, thinking, "he wouldn't be talking about rods or chains."

"He wouldn't be following no fence lines, either," the lawyer said, with a cackle that quickly became a hacking coughing fit that frightened Jill momentarily. Fearing that she might still be in the office when the man suffered a heart attack, she broke off her interview and quickly made her farewells.

She found another park bench and sat down to regroup. What could she make of what she had learned? For that matter, had she actually learned anything at all? A man whose putative profession was oil exploration was apparently interested in exploring on land, rather than offshore where most exploration in the area was being conducted. Did he have some secret information that he hoped to exploit?

Jill did not pretend to be expert in oil exploration, but it seemed unlikely to her that a man who (apparently) rarely left his office would be in possession of knowledge of which an entire industry was unaware. If the seekers of oil were not searching for oil deposits on the land nearby, there was probably a good reason.

So what was Roger Van Dorn searching for, if not for oil? And did it really matter? Her interest, after all, was not in Harriet's father, except as it might bear on Harriet herself. She could see no reason so far to pursue the matter further.

But, on the other hand, she had come quite some distance from Natchez, and it would be foolish to return before exhausting all—or at least a few more—possibilities. Perhaps the land records would tell her something. If Van Dorn was seeking real estate, it might be interesting to see if he actually bought some and, if so, where he bought it.

She assumed it was too late to visit the land offices now. She would need to stay overnight. Then she could devote all, or most, of the day to a diligent search through the records.

This, at last, was something she could do as well as anyone.

BROWNSVILLE, PENNSYLVANIA

SPRING 1816

It was the object of some derision, this new steamboat.

It looked like no boat—steam or not—that anyone had ever seen. It *did* resemble, however slightly, the flat-bottomed *pirogues* that Louisiana Frenchmen used to pole along their shallow *bayous*, although few of the layabouts around the Ohio River waterfront had more than a passing acquaintance with Louisiana.

The resemblance to pirogues began and ended with Shreve's boat's shallow, flat-bottom hull, for above the hull, Henry Miller Shreve had built a substantial superstructure like nothing seen before. Some thought it more resembled a wedding cake than a boat.

The main features of the lower deck—for there were *two* decks—were the massive steam engines themselves. There were two of those, as well; no previous steam vessel had had more than one. How could a steamboat captain keep these two engines working together? Previous steamboats had placed the engine in the hold, with the piston pumping vertically. Shreve had placed the engines on their sides, with the pistons operating horizontally.

In yet another departure from tradition, the dual engines powered two separate paddlewheels, located midway along the hull, rather than a single paddlewheel at the stern. And that was the strangest feature of all, for instead of the one enormous sternwheel that most steamboat men had employed, Shreve had built *two* such wheels and had placed one on each side of the vessel. This was absurd, and how Shreve would keep two wheels operating together was difficult to imagine.

And what advantage could be derived from two sidewheels that a single sternwheel could not provide? If one of those engines were to prove more powerful than the other, how could the crew maintain a straight course? Wouldn't the boat simply go in circles?

The upper deck, apparently, was designated for passengers or cargo. The pilot, it appeared, would steer the craft from the upper deck. Some of those bystanders, few of whom had ever made the downstream journey to New Orleans, marveled at this curiosity. The pilot seemed a long way from the rudder and the paddlewheels.

Shreve heard the talk, but if it bothered him he did not let it show. He thought he knew what he was doing. Time would tell, of course. It always did.

Shreve named the boat the *Washington*. His father, despite his Quaker upbringing, had fought alongside the general in the American Revolution and had instilled in his children an abiding respect for the man. Clearly, Shreve expected great things from his creation.

The spectators waited eagerly to see this contraption of Shreve's in action, but they were in for a long wait. For several days after its launch, the *Washington* lay quietly at its mooring awaiting cargo. However eager Shreve might have been to show off with his new creation, he was, first of all, a businessman. He could not afford to sail without revenue. He had partners, impatient for a return on their investment, and creditors, whose patience was also limited.

When at last the boat was ready to sail, a crowd gathered once more. As the boat eased away from the dock into the river channel, a ripple of astonishment passed through the onlookers.

The dual-engine design that had been the source of so much merriment turned out not to be the impediment that the scoffers had predicted. Far from it, in fact: the two engines—essentially identical in design and construction—worked harmoniously together.

And when it became necessary, the dual engines could work at cross purposes—one engine powering forward with the other working in reverse—which had the happy advantage of reducing the boat's turning radius. Sternwheelers always had difficulty whenever it was necessary to alter course, but Shreve's new boat had no such problem.

The *Washington* began its downstream journey amid cheers and excitement, but it did not go far. Only a few miles downstream, it pulled into a landing and took on cargo. It stayed there for two days. Then the fires were lit again, and the boilers built up steam for the journey to New Orleans.

Then, disaster struck.

While preparations were under way for the departure, the river current caught the boat. The *Washington's* stern swung toward midstream. The crew hurried to throw out a kedge anchor to arrest this movement. The effort occupied the attentions of the entire crew, Shreve included.

As the crew struggled to arrest the drift, one of the boat's boilers exploded. Gallons of scalding water gushed from the vessel, drenching and injuring the crew, and igniting a number of onboard fires.

Shreve and his pilot were fortunate; they were blown overboard. When he surfaced, Shreve could hear the agonized screams of the injured crew members. When he climbed aboard again, the magnitude of the disaster became all too clear.

Eight men were dead. Many more, judging by the extent of their injuries, were probably beyond hope. And the boat—his beloved boat—had burned almost to the water line.

But as he walked the deck, Shreve began to see a ray of hope. One boiler had exploded and would need to be repaired or replaced, but the other was intact. And while he sympathized with the families of his crew, he knew that a new crew would be simple enough to find. The sense of adventure, the opportunities to see New Orleans—the fabled city of Frenchmen and sin—and the pay: these inducements would overcome whatever fears might arise from this calamity. Americans were like that.

And *someone* would succeed in establishing steam power on the western rivers. It would not be Fulton and Livingston. It might very well be Shreve. Certainly, no one else understood the difficulties—and the possibilities—as well as he.

Even amid the anguished cries of the injured and the smoldering wreckage of his steamboat, Shreve concluded that all was not lost. The *Washington could* be salvaged. It *could* sail again, and it *would* reach New Orleans. More important, it would *return* from New Orleans—with cargo.

WASHINGTON, DC

THE TWELFTH DAY

The phone call came shortly before the dinner hour, and his landlady knocked on the Man of God's door to inform him. When he descended the stairs, she handed him a cordless handset. He took it to the dining room of the boarding house and shut the door for privacy.

"Hello," he said. A silly greeting, he had always thought, but he dared not say anything more committal. He had no doubt there were ears pressed to the door, seeking whatever scraps of information they might glean. Boarding houses were like that.

"We have the merchandise you requested," said the voice on the line.

"Good," said the Man of God. "Everything I asked for?"

"Almost everything," the voice said. "Some items you'll have to acquire down there. Nothing too difficult, though."

"How should I arrange to pick it up?"

"You'll need to come to us," said the voice. "This isn't something we can put in the mail."

"I'll come tomorrow, then. I'm eager to get started."

"Rent a car," the voice said. "Or a truck. You don't want to carry this stuff on the train."

"All right," said the Man of God.

He took careful notes as the voice told him where to go to get the "merchandise." After hanging up, he tore the sheet of paper from the notepad by the telephone. Then he tore out several succeeding sheets so that someone could not run a pencil lead over the next sheet of paper and determine his message by deciphering the imprint he left behind. This was too important a matter to have it compromised, especially at this stage.

He returned to his room and put on a light jacket, because springtime in Washington could still be cool at night. He descended the stairs again and told his landlady that he was going out.

"I was just about to put supper on the table," she said in an injured tone.

"I'm sorry. This is important, and I must go. I'll grab a bite while I'm out," he replied. She protested, but he was already on his way out the door.

It was two blocks to the Metro station, and he used the time to decide which way he would go. He knew there were car rental offices downtown, but he suspected that they would be closed for the day. That left the railroad station or the airport. The airport, he decided, would be the better bet; the rental agencies would be open later, to accommodate incoming travelers, and there would be a greater selection from which to choose. He would choose the cheapest car he could find, as long as it had seats for two people and a back seat on which to secure his cargo. It would not be wise to drive his own vehicle.

A tremor of excitement coursed through him, but he pushed it down. At last the plan was again in motion, but there were still so many things that could go wrong. It was essential that he maintain his concentration on the ultimate objective.

There was no time for emotion now. He must remain cool-headed and calm. He had work to do.

THE OHIO RIVER BELOW
LOUISVILLE

AUTUMN 1816

The *Washington* was on the river again by September. Shreve had worked tirelessly through the summer, placating frightened investors, acquiring the raw materials, and supervising the reconstruction of the shell of his riverboat.

This time, to the surprise of many (and the consternation of some), the launch was uneventful. The *Washington* moved smoothly away from the shore and began the long journey to New Orleans.

Shreve had feared that news of the boiler explosion and fire during the previous spring would have the effect of scaring away potential customers and passengers when he finally was ready for his maiden downstream voyage. He need not have worried. If prospective passengers seemed reluctant to join him, that reluctance did not extend to their cargo. Consequently, he was kept busy at nearly every port along the way, loading goods bound for New Orleans and across the ocean.

Furs came aboard in abundance, as well as farm products of all sorts: beef packed in brine, corn in all its various forms—meal, whole unshucked ears, and (of course), whiskey—and vegetables for the table. In the past, an attempt to send perishable products over so great a distance would have been thought ridiculous. Now, although some still were dubious, a number of enterprising yeomen took a chance.

The downstream voyage was largely without incident. Steamboats were still a novelty in these upriver communities, so large crowds appeared at the riverside whenever the *Washington* pulled in and dropped its mooring lines. But there was little of the jeering and laughter that had greeted him on his previous journey. Steam, it appeared, had arrived.

NEWARK, NEW JERSEY

THE THIRTEENTH DAY

The instructions on the phone had sent the Man of God to a part of Newark with which he was unfamiliar. He had followed the directions carefully, he thought, but he had missed a turn or something, and had spent nearly an hour finding his way. He had arrived at his destination about ten minutes after the agreed-upon time, and the man at the warehouse had been about to leave.

"You're lucky I was still here," he said. The Man of God did not respond; it was against his principles to apologize.

"This is all you got?" said the man at the warehouse, eyeing his rental car.

"I didn't think I needed anything bigger," said the Man of God. "Isn't this big enough?"

"Yeah, we're only talking about ten pounds. It'll fit in your trunk, easy. I'm just surprised. Usually people bring a truck."

"It's not going to blow up, is it? I thought this stuff was pretty stable."

"Oh, it's stable, all right. You'll need a blasting cap or something like that to set it off. You put a match to it, it'll burn. In Vietnam they used to break off chunks and set them on fire to cook their meals. But it'll take more than that to explode it."

He was on the road again in minutes. At first, considering his cargo, he drove slowly and carefully, but he realized after a while that he was attracting attention by slowing down the traffic around him. So he picked up his speed to match the traffic.

Caution to the winds, he thought. *I don't have to worry about it. God will provide.*

He reached Washington by nightfall without incident.

CONCORDIA PARISH

THE THIRTEENTH DAY

"I've run out of ideas," said Levesque.

He had entered Sprenkel's office almost furtively, which Sprenkel had never seen him do before, and slumped into the chair across the desk. Sprenkel was shocked—no, not shocked, precisely—but certainly surprised. Levesque was not given to timidity or embarrassment, but a quick glance at his face confirmed that he was uncomfortable with whatever he had to say.

"What sort of ideas?" Sprenkel said mildly. No need to make things worse, at least until he knew what the problem was.

"It's the airfield thing," Levesque said, after a minute. "I've looked all over, widened my circle to about four-hundred miles, and I haven't found squat."

"No other airfields?"

"Oh, lots of airfields. Just none that would fit our requirements. They're either too beat-up to land on or take off from, or they're too carefully watched. Somebody lives on the property, or they live nearby and have a clear sightline to the field, or the area is too built-up."

"Surprising," Sprenkel said. And disheartening, too, he thought, but didn't say.

"And the other thing is lights," Levesque said. "You can't make an instrument landing at a field without an ILS system, so you'd have to do it visually. And if you're doing it at night, you're gonna need lights. It wouldn't be so hard in the daytime, but…"

"But somebody would see you in the daytime," Sprenkel said. "I get it. I'm kicking myself that I didn't think of that before."

"Well, it doesn't matter now. We've just got to figure out something else. Maybe they're not using an airplane after all. Maybe they really *did* carry the girl's body from the road to the levee."

"Maybe," Sprenkel said.

He didn't believe it, though. The extent of the injuries to Harriet Van Dorn's body, the distance from the road to the levee, the absence of footprints in the soft earth despite the recent rains, all pointed toward a single conclusion: the girl had been dropped from a considerable height, probably while she was still living, and an aircraft of some sort was the only way he could imagine that it could have been done.

"What about fixed base operators?" he said, finally.

"You mean those general aviation terminals at the big airports?" Levesque said. "I guess we can check it out, but I can't see that they'd tolerate somebody loading a dead body onto an airplane right under their noses."

"I don't think so, either, but she could've been alive when they boarded. They'd still have to get permission from the control tower in order to takeoff," Sprenkel said. "But we ought to check it out, anyway."

Levesque left to begin the task, and Sprenkel turned back to the paperwork that seemed to breed like rabbits. It was going to be a late night again, and the accumulation of red tape that was threatening to overwhelm him. In Baltimore he would have resented all the administrative duties that kept him away from home, sometimes until the early morning hours. But here... what was there to go home to?

VIDALIA, LOUISIANA, CONCORDIA PARISH

LATER THAT DAY

"Sheriff, sorry to bother you, but I think our paths are crossing again."

It took a minute for Sprenkel to recognize her voice, which he had last heard two weeks previously.

"Sergeant Graziano? It's no bother, really. Happy to hear from you. What's up?"

He could hear her sighing heavily.

"You remember the man who turned up dead in the French Quarter? The one you came down here to ask about?"

"Angelo Sweet."

"That's right. Well, this is a little embarrassing, but it's beginning to look like this Mr. Sweet doesn't exist."

"I know," Sprenkel said.

"You already know? How…"

"I went looking for him in Shreveport. Couldn't find even a trace of anybody by that name. How'd *you* come to this conclusion?"

"We did something similar," she said. "We were looking for next-of-kin. Turns out that there aren't any."

"Because there was never an Angelo Sweet," Sprenkel said.

"Oh, there *was* an Angelo Sweet, all right. He was from Slidell. He was killed in Vietnam back in the seventies. Fairly early in the seventies—seventy-two, seventy-three, somewhere about then."

"Only child, no surviving relatives," Sprenkel speculated.

"Right. There *was* a cousin—second cousin—over in Yazoo City," Graziano said. "He confirmed that the Angelo Sweet who was killed in Vietnam in the seventies wasn't likely to turn up as a fresh corpse in New Orleans more than thirty years later."

Sprenkel found himself imagining Graziano at her phone, unconsciously brushing a strand of hair from her eyes, as she had done frequently during their meeting in New Orleans. Her hair was dark, almost black, with a few tentative streaks of gray. She wore it short, neatly parted, almost mannish, but there was something about her face that....

He shook his head to dispel the image. He had not found her particularly appealing at their one meeting in the office of the medical examiner, but now....

Was desperation beginning to set in? *I've been too long without feminine contact*, he thought. His long period of self-imposed celibacy had not quenched the desires that he had tried so hard to bury under a mountain of work. He had moved away from Baltimore, and from Diane, to put her out of his reach—for his own sake as much as for hers. Of course, *she* hadn't chosen celibacy. Her husband had forgiven her, had taken her back. No doubt they would have a rocky time of it, but they would work it out. Somehow.

Giselle had been less forgiving. Sprenkel's marriage had been over long before....

"...around noon or so, if I can get away from the office on time," Graziano was saying, and Sprenkel realized he had not been paying attention. From the sound of things, Graziano was planning on coming up to see him. What had he missed?

He took a deep breath.

"Well, you'll be welcome. We'll be happy to see you, and we'll give you all the cooperation we can."

"I wasn't concerned about that," she said. "I knew you would. I'm just sorry to have to impose on you like this."

"No problem," he said. "But do you really think you'll find something about Angelo Sweet up here? I think we've combed this area pretty good."

"It's a little more complicated than that," she said. "I'll explain it all when I get there."

MORGAN CITY, LOUISIANA

THE THIRTEENTH DAY

Roger Van Dorn, Jill discovered, had been quite active.

It hadn't been apparent, at first. Van Dorn's name wasn't in the records of land transactions. But she noticed that a rather large number of parcels had been purchased by, or optioned to, a corporation called Madeleine Enterprises. The name didn't register with her at first, until she recalled that Madeleine was the name of Harriet's mother and the name Harriet had apparently used for prostitution. It would be a logical name for Van Dorn's shell corporation, if he wanted to cover his tracks.

There was nothing in the records that she could see, that listed the officers of Madeleine Enterprises. She suspected she'd have to go to Baton Rouge, the state capital, for that information. It would be there; a corporation doing business in Louisiana would have to register with the state. But would it be worth the trouble for her to seek it?

In the meantime, she thought, she could take a look at the land that Madeleine Enterprises had so carefully, and furtively, acquired.

It took the better part of a day to identify all the parcels in the parish records and transfer that information to her own map. When she was finished, she came out into twilight. The last pinks of sunset were fading, and the gray night was approaching rapidly.

She would not have time to investigate all the parcels; she had to be back in Natchez in the morning for a class. But a couple of the parcels— one purchased, one optioned—were on her way home. She could at least take a look at them on her way north. It would be getting dark quickly, but perhaps she would be able to make some rough assessment in the time remaining before the last vestiges of daylight were gone.

The parcels, however, were a disappointment: several acres of scrub land, much of it marsh, far from either commercial or residential development. If location was the most important element in determining the value of real estate, as she had often heard, these parcels seemed completely illogical. There was a road, of sorts, but it would need to be upgraded considerably if it were to handle much commercial traffic.

Worst of all, these parcels were nearly a mile from the river, and the Atchafalaya was Morgan City's lifeblood.

Their only saving grace, to Jill's eyes, was that they abutted each other. If this area ever *did* become valuable, Madeleine Enterprises would be in an enviable position.

She could not, however, imagine any circumstance that would make it a possibility.

NATCHEZ, MISSISSIPPI

THE FOURTEENTH DAY

"I guess I owe you an apology," Sergeant Graziano said. "I didn't believe that your case had anything to do with ours."

"But now you've changed your mind?" Sprenkel said.

"We've had some new information," Graziano said. "And it's pointing in this direction."

"What sort of information?"

Graziano was absently twisting her hair again, the way she had during that earlier interview in New Orleans. *A nervous habit*, Sprenkel thought, and he wondered what might have made her nervous. Admitting to a mistake?

"You asked me if any hookers had turned up missing recently," Graziano said. "I promised that I'd look into it."

"And somebody was missing?"

"Not as far as I can tell. Like I told you, we don't exactly maintain a census, but…"

"Then what?"

"Ever hear of something called Old River?" she said, after a moment.

They were in a booth in a restaurant in Natchez. Sergeant Graziano had taken a room in a hotel on the Mississippi side of the river. She had suggested that they meet for lunch and asked for suggestions. Sprenkel had none, but he asked Levesque, who seemed quite knowledgeable on the subject.

Sprenkel found himself wedged in uncomfortably next to Levesque, who was a large man. Graziano was facing them across the table.

"Old River," she prompted. "Does that ring any bells?"

"Hell, yeah," Levesque said. "It's in our backyard, in a manner of speaking."

"What does Old River have to do with the alleged Angelo Sweet?" Sprenkel said. "Or for that matter, what does it have to do with our dead hooker?"

"I don't know, to tell you the truth," Graziano said. "But one of our detectives busted up a meth operation and turned up some notes referring to Old River. The notes also referred to an A. Sweet. He seemed to be right in the middle of whatever was going down."

"And our dead prostitute? Does she fit into this business somewhere?"

Graziano thought for a moment. "I don't know. Maybe she doesn't, but this group used prostitutes for distributing their product."

"And Old River? What does that have to do with anything?"

"I don't know that, either," Graziano said. "But there's a lot of back and forth discussion in the notes about the price of explosives. We don't like the sound of it."

"I can understand that," Sprenkel said. "But Old River? What's the connection?"

"Maybe there isn't one, but the notes mention Old River and explosives almost in the same sentence, and they appear together in two or three different notes."

"If you were going to blow something up," Levesque said, after a moment, "Old River would make quite a splash. Maybe we should take a little field trip down that way and check things out."

"I sort of know where it is, in a general way," said Graziano. "But where is Old River, precisely? In relation to us right here?"

"Well, we're on the Mississippi side right now," Levesque said. "But if we were across the river, in Vidalia, Old River would be about due south of us. Route 15 would take you right to it. Right over it, in fact."

"How far would that be?"

"Top of my head—sixty, seventy miles."

"An hour from here," Graziano said.

"A little less, the way I drive," Levesque said.

Graziano thought about this.

"Let's do it," she said.

Sprenkel and Levesque made arrangements for a trip to Old River, with Sergeant Graziano, the following morning. Sprenkel returned to his office to work on paperwork, although he was beginning to doubt that he would ever be caught up.

At about two o'clock, he received a phone call.

"Sheriff Sprenkel? This is Jill Winston."

"Miss Winston! How are you? I'd been meaning to call you, but…"

"You had?" She sounded incredulous.

"I feel bad about… that evening. I've been meaning to apologize for the way I acted."

"Actually," she said, "I should be apologizing to you. I didn't mean to be so aggressive, forcing myself on you."

"You didn't force yourself on me, and I certainly wasn't offended. It's just that my life's a little complicated right now. I don't want to lay it all on you, though."

"I don't want to pry," she said. "But if there's anything I can do…"

"Thank you. Maybe someday. But I don't think that's why you called."

"No, it isn't. I found something I thought might be useful to you in your investigation… about Harriet."

"What did you find?"

"I'm afraid I did some poking around on my own," she said. "I know we… civilians aren't supposed to do that, but…."

"I'm not ashamed of taking help from civilians, Miss Winston. What did you find?"

"It's Jill, please."

"Okay. Jill it is. What did you find while you were poking around?"

"I was curious about Harriet's father. I'm not entirely sure *why* I was curious about him, but…."

"Okay. You were curious," he said, as patiently as he could muster. "What did you find?"

"Well, I went to Morgan City, where Harriet grew up. At first, I was just looking for any trace of her that I might be able to find. That trail went cold pretty quickly, so I decided to look for records of her father, instead. I thought an adult male surely would leave tracks… records of transactions, driver's licenses, that sort of thing."

"You probably could have done that from home."

"Maybe so. I didn't really think about that; I just wanted to get out of the apartment."

"So you found something of interest?"

"I didn't realize it until I read in the newspaper about the murder of Harriet's mother and father. A week ago, wasn't it?"

"That sounds about right."

"Well, Harriet's father has been buying up land around Morgan City."

"Really? That's interesting. How much land are we talking about?"

"About a couple hundred acres, as nearly as I can tell. But that's not the most interesting thing."

"And that is?"

"He made his most recent purchase just a week ago. *After* he was murdered!"

Sprenkel was silent for a moment.

"Miss Winston… Jill," Sprenkel said thoughtfully. "Would you happen to be free tomorrow?"

"Why, Sheriff, are you asking me out?" she said, demurely. "Like on a date?"

"Well, I suppose so, in a manner of speaking," he said. "I'd like to take you along on a little field trip we have planned."

NATCHEZ, MISSISSIPPI

THE FIFTEENTH DAY

Graziano had not been pleased by the delay in setting out for Old River, particularly when she learned that the delay was occasioned by the detour to pick up Jill.

"This isn't a pleasure trip. Sheriff," she said, testily. "I'm on official business here. I resent your bringing your girlfriend along."

"She's not my girlfriend," Sprenkel said. "She's the roommate of our dead hooker. I think she may be able to contribute some information that will help us in our investigation—our *murder* investigation."

"I think you're reaching," Graziano said. "That's pretty lame."

"Humor me," Sprenkel said. Levesque, at the wheel, stared quietly ahead.

The trip progressed in a sullen atmosphere. Sprenkel sat in the front passenger seat of the police cruiser. Graziano sat behind Levesque and stared out the window. Jill, after a few forced attempts at conversation, gave up the effort and stared out her window.

They left Vidalia and turned south. The landscape hardly changed: flat land on both sides of the highway with an occasional service station or retail store. At last, the Old River superstructure appeared.

Levesque pulled the car over to the shoulder and killed the ignition.

"Well, this is it," he said.

He turned to Graziano, sitting behind him.

"Ring any bells?" he said.

"Not so far," she replied. "I'm going to get out and look around."

Jill and the others followed. They stood on the river bank staring at the mass of concrete and steel.

"This used to be a meander," Levesque said.

"What's a meander?" Jill asked.

"It's a bend in the river," Graziano said.

"Down here," Levesque said, "the river isn't fixed in its course so much. It wanders all over the place, looking for a shorter route to the gulf, or softer land or a steeper grade, that would let it get there faster. So it's always wandering around, searching for a better way to go. Sometimes a bend will silt up and get cut off from the main channel. That's a meander."

"This looks like a dam," Jill said, indicating the superstructure. "Is it a dam?"

"It's a dam," Sprenkel said. "Sort of. It's called the Old River Control Structure."

"Why is it here?"

"It controls the Mississippi," Levesque said. "It keeps the Mississippi from changing course."

"Why would the Mississippi change course? It's been here forever." Jill said. "How old is New Orleans, now? Three hundred years?"

"About that, I guess."

"And the Mississippi was here then, or else they wouldn't have built New Orleans where it is. So how can the river change course?"

"Well, it can take a couple thousand years, sometimes, but it *does* happen. And I guess it's overdue."

"Actually," Graziano said, "the river changed course a long time ago—about fifty years ago. Right here."

"That's the reason for this river control business," Levesque said. "It lets a little water pass through, to protect the wetlands along the Atchafalaya, while keeping most of the Mississippi in the old channel."

Jill was silent as she pondered this bit of information. Rivers *did* change course on occasion—she knew that—but the Mississippi? The river was so big, so seemingly relentless; it was difficult to imagine it moving somewhere else. And if the river *did* choose to go elsewhere, it was just as hard to imagine that human beings could prevent it. Surely not with this puny pile of steel and concrete.

"Why would the river change course?" she said finally. "You make it sound like it's some sort of petulant little boy, throwing tantrums when things don't go his way."

"Well, yeah, sort of," said Levesque.

Jill looked at Sprenkel, who merely shrugged.

"He's the expert," Sprenkel said, indicating Levesque.

The road now took them over the top of the dam, and Jill could see a barge and towboat down below. The tow was passing through on its way from the main channel of the Mississippi to… where? She realized suddenly that she had traveled this road before, on her trip to Morgan City.

I've been there. Strange. she thought.

"I refuse to go all the way to Morgan City," Sergeant Graziano said. "There's no point to it. I've no evidence that Angelo Sweet was *ever* in Morgan City."

"Wait a minute," Jill said. "Who is this Angelo person you keep talking about?"

"He was a man who was killed in New Orleans," Sprenkel said. "Sergeant Graziano has been investigating his murder, and she thinks there's a connection with the death of your flat mate."

"What sort of connection?"

"We don't know," Graziano said. "His name came up in the arrests of some suspected terrorists. This group used prostitutes to deliver drugs, and your roommate was…"

"A prostitute, yes, I know. I still can't believe it."

"The connection still seems a little weak," Sprenkel said. "If it wasn't for the DNA evidence, I doubt that we'd bother. But semen from this Angelo guy was found in Harriet's body."

"She had sex with this guy not long before she died," Levesque said. "So there was obviously some sort of relationship there, even if it was only a business transaction."

"Why don't you show her this guy's picture?" Sprenkel said to Graziano. "Maybe it's somebody she's seen around."

Graziano shrugged and produced the picture from the man's driver's license. Jill glanced at the photograph. Then she glanced at it again. This time, she studied it closely.

"Oh, God," she said. It was said so softly that Sprenkel almost didn't hear it.

"Someone you recognize?" Sprenkel said. "A friend, maybe? A classmate?"

"He's a little old for a college student," Levesque observed. "Even a graduate student."

"I think I know him. I never met him, and I only saw his picture that one time, but I'm pretty sure," Jill said.

"Where did you see it?" Sprenkel said.

"It was on Harriet's desk," she said. "She said it was a family picture. His real name is… was Roger Van Dorn. He's Harriet's father."

"What?" said Sergeant Graziano. "That can't be!"

"The photo disappeared from the apartment," Jill said. "So I can't be certain. But it certainly *looks* like the man Harriet said was her father."

"This man had sexual intercourse with the woman who… with your roommate," Graziano said.

"Not unheard of," Levesque said quietly.

"But the DNA would have shown they were related," Graziano said. "That would have jumped right out at us! The DNA showed there was no relationship at all."

"He certainly *looks* like the same man," Jill said.

"Could your roommate have been adopted?" Sprenkel said. "That could explain the difference in DNA."

"I don't know that, either," Jill said. "I just remember looking at the photograph on Harriet's desk, and I remember her telling me that it was a picture of her family. And she pointed to this man and called him her father."

"And you're sure it's the same man?" Graziano persisted.

"As sure as I can be without having the picture in front of me," Jill said. "Like I said, the photograph disappeared from the apartment. I just assumed the police had taken it."

"*We* didn't take it," Sprenkel said. "And I don't remember seeing it among the evidence that the Natchez police collected, either."

"When did you see it last?" Graziano asked.

Jill thought. "I'm not sure. I think it was before I learned that Harriet was dead. Maybe a day or two before that."

"A day or two."

"Or more. I don't know; I didn't think about it seriously until I realized she wouldn't be coming back."

"Could your roommate have taken it herself?" Sprenkel asked. "Could she have returned to the apartment one day while you were out?"

"Of course. But why would she do that, unless she wasn't planning to return? And I don't think that's the case. She didn't take her clothes, or anything else that I can think of."

"I don't know," Sprenkel admitted. "It doesn't make sense, yet. But I bet it will."

PART TWO

The "control of nature" is a phrase conceived in arrogance, born of the Neanderthal age of biology and the convenience of man.

—Rachel Carson (Silent Spring, *1962*)

THE WESTERN RIVERS

AUTUMN 1816

The *Washington* was on the river again by September. Shreve had worked tirelessly through the summer, placating frightened investors, acquiring the raw materials, and supervising the reconstruction of the shell of his riverboat.

This time, to the surprise of many (and the consternation of some), the launch was uneventful. The *Washington* moved smoothly away from the shore and began the long journey to New Orleans.

Shreve had feared that news of the boiler explosion and fire during the previous spring would have the effect of scaring away potential customers and passengers when he finally was ready for his maiden downstream voyage. He need not have worried; if prospective passengers seemed reluctant to join him, their reluctance did not extend to prospective shippers. He was kept busy at nearly every port along the way, loading goods bound for New Orleans and, from there, across the ocean.

Much of the cargo was cotton, a commodity in great demand on both sides of the Atlantic. Furs were also important, as well as farm products of all sorts: beef packed in brine, corn in all its various forms—meal, whole unhusked ears, and (of course) whiskey—and vegetables for the table. In the past, any attempt to send perishable products over so great a distance would have been thought absurd. Now, although some still were dubious, a number of enterprising merchants took the chance.

The downstream voyage was largely without incident. Steamboats were still a novelty in these upriver communities, and large crowds appeared at the riverside whenever the *Washington* pulled in and dropped its mooring lines. But there was little of the jeering and laughter that had greeted him on his previous journey.

In New Orleans, of course, the Fulton-Livingston monopoly still lay in wait.

VIDALIA, LOUISIANA

THE FIFTEENTH DAY

"There's a Mr. Eastwood here to see you, sir."

"Clint?"

"I didn't ask him his first name, sir. I'll go ask him now."

"Never mind," Sprenkel said. "Just show him in."

Eastwood, he thought. *That was the name of the....*

"Good morning, Sheriff. Good of you to see me on such short notice," said the visitor, whom Sprenkel recognized from their brief meeting in the parking lot... one week ago, was it?

"Good morning, sir. Find your fishing hole?"

"Nice of you to remember, sir," said the man who called himself Eastwood. "No, I'm afraid I've been too busy to go fishing, lately. Press of business, you know."

"That reminds me," Sprenkel said. "I've been meaning to ask you: what, precisely, *is* your business, Mr. Eastwood?"

The hesitation was almost unnoticeable.

"Well, sir, you might say I'm a salesman. Pharmaceutical products, among others. I'm on the road quite a lot."

"Who do you sell to?" Sprenkel asked. "Hospitals? Private practices?"

"Both," Eastwood said. "It keeps me on the move. I've found that I just don't have time for leisure pursuits. I'm new to this job. Maybe my situation will improve after a while."

"Well, good luck to you. Now, what can I do for you?"

Nothing."

"Nothing?"

"There's nothing I need at present," Eastwood replied. "I've found it useful over the years to pay a call now and then on local officials, to inform them of my presence. It allays concerns, I find—greases the skids, you might say."

"So this is... what... a courtesy call?

"Exactly! A courtesy call! There's no cause for concern. I'm simply paying my respects. Thank you for seeing me; I realize I may be interrupting a busy day, and for this I must apologize."

"Always happy to meet a constituent," Sprenkel said. He thought: *What a puzzling visit!*

NEW ORLEANS

AUTUMN 1816

In the past, Henry Miller Shreve thought, a visitor's first sighting of New Orleans would have been the spire of the cathedral. That was the case no more.

Today, even before the cathedral, the eye beheld a forest: a forest of ship's masts clustered at the landing below the city, all awaiting cargo for export—mostly cotton. King Cotton, as it was commonly called, had made this little settlement— a largely French-speaking outpost that occupied the first high ground above the mouth of the river—into a major seaport.

There were fortunes to be made here, assuming, of course, that the Fulton-Livingston monopoly did not get him first. Shreve could not see the representatives of the monopoly awaiting him at the landing, but he knew they were there. Most assuredly they were there, and now that the war was over they would be able to move against him without official opposition.

Shreve had taken precautions, in concert with lawyer A. L. Duncan, but it was likely to be a close-run thing. Victory was not assured.

The *Washington* moved into position at the riverbank, and his crew secured the boat to its mooring. The great paddlewheels ceased their thrashing, and the two steam boilers were shut down. For a few moments the eerie silence was broken only by the popping sound of cooling metal, a sound that Shreve was slowly becoming accustomed to at every stop. It had taken him some time to adjust to; it was unlike any sound on a keelboat.

The gangplank was lowered, and he stepped onto dry land. As anticipated, the officious form of Edward Livingston was bustling forward already, a sheaf of Important Official Papers clutched in his right hand. Livingston was accompanied, Shreve noted, by two of the city's gendarmes, bearing muskets.

Loaded for bear, he thought. Livingston is making a show of force to convince me of his seriousness of purpose. Well, he shall soon see that I am serious, also.

"Mr. Shreve, I assume you know why I am here," Livingston said, waving his papers for emphasis.

"*Captain* Shreve," Shreve corrected. "Yes, I know. We have trod this path before."

"But this time we are no longer at war," Livingston said. "Your General Jackson has left the city. I present you with this order from the court, which empowers me to seize your vessel for violation of our monopoly. The price for redeeming your boat will be ten thousand dollars. You are now at my mercy, sir."

"Hardly that," Shreve said. "I see Lawyer Duncan hurrying this way. You know Lawyer Duncan, I believe?"

"I know him well," Livingston said. "But the law is on my side now. He can do nothing for you."

He said this in a loud voice, as if to ensure that Duncan, who was now arriving, would hear and be afraid.

"Perhaps not," Duncan said. "On the other hand, perhaps Captain Shreve is not as helpless as you assume."

He placed a new sheaf of papers in Livingston's hand. The monopolist gave them only a cursory glance.

"What is this?" Livingston said.

"What is it? Why, it is an order of the court, which prohibits any actions that might adversely affect the interests of a party in a civil lawsuit."

"And you are serving this on me? Since I am in the right, you should serve this on your client."

"Ah, well, who is right and who is wrong is a matter for the courts to decide," Duncan blandly replied. "However, my duty to my client requires me to protect his interests, pending the court's decision."

"The court's decision is a foregone conclusion," Livingston said, testily.

"We shall see, won't we?" Duncan said. "Until that time, however, I must ask you to depart this vessel. It does not, at present, belong to you."

Livingston was clearly reluctant to go, but his authorized escorts saw no reason to remain. An unruly crowd of riverboat men had gathered on the quay, shouting and hurling threats at Livingston. Facing the ire of the boatmen, who remembered Shreve's efforts during the battle for New Orleans, the official guards beat a hasty retreat. Deprived of his official backup, facing a mob ashore and an angry crew of steamboat men on the *Washington*, the monopolists' representative decided it was in his interest to retreat. Mustering as much dignity as he could, Livingston stormed off.

"What are our chances?" Shreve said when Livingston had departed. "Can we truly defeat the monopolists in court?"

"That depends on you," Duncan said. "Can you sail back up the Mississippi on steam power alone? And can you then return, with a cargo, to show that it can be done?"

"Yes."

"Then I believe we can prevail. As a matter of fact, I believe we *will* prevail. And the best thing you can do… Captain Shreve… is to get under way as soon as practicable, thereby removing yourself from Mr. Livingston's reach."

"Mr. Livingston will not go away on his own," Shreve said. "He will still be waiting when I return."

"Leave it for me to deal with Mr. Livingston," Duncan replied. "Will you do that?"

"Gladly, sir," Shreve said, smiling. "And if you would be so good as to disembark, I shall begin my departure preparations immediately."

CONCORDIA, LOUISIANA

THE FIFTEENTH DAY

"The thing is," Caulfield was saying, "I still don't know who all these people are."

"Come again?" Sprenkel said. He had been thinking about his curious meeting with Eastwood when the call had come in from the Memphis detective.

"I'm still trying to identify some of the victims in this gang shooting up here," Caulfield said. "You remember—you were there with me when we found them."

"Right, the Van Dorn family. Sorry. My mind was somewhere else."

"Except it isn't the Van Dorn family. Well, it's *Mrs*. Van Dorn, I guess. She was the woman in the hot tub. But the rest of them, we still don't have identification on them."

"I thought that was fairly obvious," Sprenkel said. "The husband's name is Roger. The son is... well, I don't think I ever heard his name, but it shouldn't be that hard to learn."

"That'd be true," Caulfield said, "if the stiff in the living room was Roger Van Dorn, which it ain't. And if the body out back was the son, which it ain't."

"Not the father or the son? I guess I don't have to ask if you're sure about that."

"We're sure who they *ain't*. But we're no closer to knowing who they are than we were when we found them. I guess I'm hoping you might have some idea. Anybody go missing down your way that might have connections up here?"

"I don't think so, and I think I'd know," Sprenkel said. "I'll check, but I don't think I'll be able to help you."

"Well, if you come up with something, give me a call," Caulfield said. "I know it's a long shot, but we're coming up dry up here."

After Caulfield disconnected, Sprenkel thought for some time about the call. A houseful of people had been murdered, but only one of them had belonged to that house. How to make sense of it?

The neighborhood had not seemed like a place where random killings were common occurrences. They sometimes happened, he knew, but it was rarely seen in such neighborhoods. People who could afford to live in those places usually had other, less messy, ways to settle disputes.

Generally—even supposedly random killings were not entirely random—the killers had a reason for selecting their particular targets. Robbery was a common motivation; perhaps the perpetrators had known about valuables of some sort that belonged to the residents. Perhaps they hadn't realized that someone would be at home.

But in that event, the Memphis police would probably know what had been taken in the robbery, and they would be checking the usual places—pawnshops, for example—where the stolen goods might turn up.

Sprenkel doubted that this was a robbery gone wrong; there were too many coincidences. Although Harriet Van Dorn's mother had been the only family member in the house when the murders occurred, it remained true that Harriet had herself been killed at about the same time, several hundred miles away. And if Jill was correct, the man who had been killed in New Orleans—who went by "Angelo Sweet"—was actually Roger Van Dorn.

And where was the brother? They had assumed that the young man who had been killed attempting an escape had been the brother. Now, it appeared, he was not. Who was he? And... where was the man for whom he had been mistaken? He might be the only surviving member of the family.

And he might, Sprenkel thought, just might be the murderer of all the others. That was a depressing thought.

NEW ORLEANS

MARCH 1817

Henry Miller Shreve—*Captain* Henry Miller Shreve—saw the ship's masts clustered below the spire of the cathedral once more and knew that the battle was about to begin again. But this time, he thought, the battle would be fought on more even ground. Lawyer A. L. Duncan had seen to that.

The Fulton-Livingston monopoly had been put on notice the previous autumn, when their attempt to seize Shreve's vessel had been foiled by Duncan's countermeasure. But Edward Livingston, the agent for the monopoly, had had nearly six months to devise a new stratagem.

And he had done so.

Livingston was not waiting at the quay when Shreve arrived. Instead, two other lesser representatives of the monopoly approached him as he stepped off the boat. Unlike Livingston, they greeted him cordially and invited him to a meeting.

"I was unaware that we had any business to transact," Shreve said. "We are adversaries in a legal matter, after all."

"I believe you may find it to your advantage," one of the representatives replied.

"Why did Mr. Livingston not meet me, as he always has previously" Shreve asked. "Is he ill?"

"Mr. Livingston is quite well, but we'll let him explain the situation to you."

* * * *

Edward Livingston was indeed well, which was quite apparent in his greeting at his office. Standing, moving from behind his desk, he offered his hand with a broad smile.

"Thank you for coming, Mr. Shreve. I'm sorry I could not meet you in person, for reasons that should soon become apparent to you."

"They are not clear to me at present," Shreve said.

"Of course. But as you are aware, we are adversaries in the legal arena. It is a burden to me as it must be to you, but it would not do for us to be seen meeting *ex officio*, as it were."

"I don't follow your reasoning. Civil matters are often settled out of the courtroom."

"In this case, an out-of-court settlement is not advisable."

"Then what…"

"I am prepared," Livingston said, "to offer you a fifty-percent interest in the Livingston-Fulton company."

Shreve felt the need to sit down. Fortunately, there was a chair nearby.

"Consider the opportunity, sir," Livingston was saying. "Our firm is quite profitable. You are profitable also, I do not doubt. Furthermore, you have shown remarkable ingenuity. Indeed, your vessel is—dare I say it—far superior to anything that we have in our fleet."

"I appreciate your… appreciation," Shreve said, still astounded.

"By combining our forces," Livingston went on, "we would grow even larger and more profitable…."

Shreve could see that there were advantages for him, as well. A half interest in the Fulton-Livingston firm would assure his future and enable him to pay off his creditors with interest. Moreover, he would be granted access to everyone of importance in every city along Ohio and Mississippi Rivers—indeed throughout the entire western river system. He thought of the thousands of farmers and merchants in the western states and territories, desperate for access to new markets. The latent desire for imported goods in the western states and territories meant that an enormous upstream market had been virtually untapped. The Livingston-Fulton company, or rather the Livingston-Fulton-*Shreve* company would be able to reach it.

It was an attractive offer. But something troubled him still. Something that had not been mentioned up to now.

"And what," Shreve said finally, "does the Livingston-Fulton company bring to the table?"

"Come again?"

"If the company gains my services, what can you offer in exchange?"

"Why, I should have thought it was obvious," Livingston said. "We have a monopoly."

The enormity of this took a moment to sink in. Livingston apparently saw the confusion in Shreve's expression.

"Undoubtedly, you are wondering what we would require of you, in addition to your obvious talents," he said. "You have only to instruct your attorney to lose your suit."

"To *lose* the suit?"

"The Livingston-Fulton Company cannot be seen to lose," Livingston explained with exaggerated patience. "If we were to lose, it would encourage a flood of challenges. Every man with a steamboat—every man who ever *contemplated* owning a steamboat—would sense vulnerability in our position. We would be inundated with frivolous lawsuits. Our time, and our capital, would be wholly devoted to fending off these challenges."

"I see," Shreve said. And with crystalline clarity, he *did* see.

The monopoly's days were numbered. He had wondered why the company would come to him with its offer of partnership, and now he understood. This offer was less an offer of partnership than it was a bribe—a bribe to buy him off, to discourage others from following suit. With a single maneuver the monopolists would gain his expertise in steamboat design while simultaneously scaring away predators.

Livingston was waiting eagerly for his reply.

"No, sir," Shreve said.

"No?" Livingston was clearly surprised.

Shreve was surprised, as well. He had been considering the partnership seriously. But, as he thought of it, he realized that a partnership in the Livingston-Fulton company would only be a temporary solution. The monopoly was vulnerable and would, inevitably, fail.

"I thank you for your offer," Shreve said, "but I must decline."

Livingston's expression hardened.

"You realize… this means that the suit will continue. I suggest that you consult with your attorney concerning the advisability of this decision."

"No need," Shreve said. "I shall see you in court."

* * * *

He wasted no time in preparing the *Washington* for his return trip upstream. He had little difficulty obtaining cargo.

Interestingly, he found also no shortage of passengers eager to experience the thrill of traveling in comparative luxury against the current of the river. Shreve had seen fit to outfit his vessel with unaccustomed luxury. Travel by stagecoach—really the only feasible alternative—could not compare with Shreve's floating castle.

His reception upstream was equally enthusiastic. In Louisville, the city fathers threw a colossal banquet in his honor. Merchants and travelers flocked to do business with the man whose boat had tamed the Mississippi.

Meanwhile, the Livingston-Fulton lawsuit dissolved in anticlimactic torpor when the court concluded that it had no jurisdiction and dismissed the case. Shreve learned about the decision on his return to New Orleans several weeks later.

CONCORDIA PARISH

THE FIFTEENTH DAY

So the man who was murdered in the Van Dorn house was *not* Roger Van Dorn. Perhaps Jill was right, and the man whom he had come to think of as "Angelo Sweet"—the man whom the police had found murdered in New Orleans—*was* Van Dorn, after all.

Sprenkel considered the situation. The Van Dorns were a family of four: father, mother, son, daughter. Three of the four were dead; only the son was unaccounted for.

The elusive son. Nobody knew the son, apparently. What did he look like? What was his name? What was his occupation, his place of residence, his interests?

There had been a photograph, a family photograph. Jill Winston had seen it, and now it was gone. Unless the Natchez police had confiscated it, and Sprenkel doubted that they had, it seemed to have disappeared into thin air.

In the absence of information, what should be the next step? How could he find information where none existed?

Well, information *did* exist, of course, somewhere; it was simply a matter of finding it. In a day in which electronic records were kept of nearly every transaction of every conceivable nature, it was difficult—nearly impossible, in fact—to drop off the grid entirely. There would be a record somewhere, and probably a photograph.

All he had to do now was to find it. He had a day or two of time off coming, and he was thinking it might be worthwhile to spend some of it looking for that record. And he thought he knew just the person to accompany him.

There was no time like the present. He picked up the phone and called her.

"Jill," he said when she answered. "How would you feel about another field trip?"

LOUISVILLE, KENTUCKY

DECEMBER 1826

The letter from Washington City bore the signature of Secretary of War James Barbour, and it informed Shreve that he had been appointed to the post of superintendent of the western rivers. His duties concerned a problem with which he was only too familiar.

Snags.

Shreve had prospered in the decade since he had first appeared in New Orleans. He was no longer the captain of a solitary keelboat; now he was the highly successful owner of three steamboats that conducted a lively traffic in both cargo and passengers. He had moved his family to Louisville, the better to manage his enterprises.

Thanks to Shreve's radical steamboat redesign, river traffic had grown exponentially. Because he had not bothered to patent his innovations, they were available to all without charge, and ambitious entrepreneurs had adopted them eagerly. The rivers were filled with shallow-draft vessels whose cargo and passenger decks were stacked above the hulls like tiers on a wedding cake.

And as river traffic grew, the snag problem also grew in importance.

Every man who made his livelihood on the western rivers knew the problem from painful experience. Western rivers were shallow, unlike those back east, and were prone to snags. Trees along the riverbanks washed into the river channels, where they lay in wait for unsuspecting boatmen. Snags would reach up from their watery graves to seize boatmen's vessels, rip apart their hulls, and drag them down to the river bottom. Fortunes were often lost, and lives as well.

Sometimes, trees would flourish and take root in the rich soil of the riverbed. These snags, which river men called "planters," were extremely difficult to remove.

All along the rivers, boatmen grumbled and whined about the problem. The government had financed a number of futile attempts to clear away these obstructions to commerce. Nearly everyone on the rivers felt that the problem was beyond the reach of man to solve. There were too many snags, they were rooted too deeply in the riverbeds, and they resisted all efforts at removal.

Henry Miller Shreve did not share the general consensus; he had a different view of the matter. Moreover, he had a solution, and it was a radical departure from all those previous efforts.

His concept was a vessel of his own design, a "snag boat." He proposed building a vessel with two hulls, with a massive iron ram suspended between them below the water line. The ram would be propelled by steam to pull up—or, if necessary, to cut down—underwater obstructions. Once they had been removed, a steam-powered saw on board the boat would cut them up and let the current take them downstream.

Shreve had proposed this to the national government before, in response to requests for such proposals. His proposal had not been accepted, or even acknowledged.

Now the Secretary of War was appointing Shreve to the post of "superintendent of the western rivers," at a salary of five thousand dollars, with the primary duty of clearing snags.

The salary was less than an industrious river captain could make in a single New Orleans trip. The appointment, moreover, did not provide funds for building his snag boat. The government did not, apparently, have confidence in such a novel concept as a steam-powered vessel to rip up embedded trees. He was expected to hire laborers—or impress slave labor—to do the job by hand, an approach that had been tried repeatedly without the slightest success.

The fact that John Quincy Adams was now President might have been a factor in the government's indifference to his proposal; Shreve had been an early and ardent supporter of Andrew Jackson. Still, the government must be desperate since they had eventually turned to him.

Well, thought Shreve, *if I must build the boat myself, then I must.*

It would not be the first time he had gone his own way, at his own expense. He suspected it would not be the last.

NATCHEZ, MISSISSIPPI

THE SIXTEENTH DAY

"I'm so excited!" Jill said. "This *is* like a date! I can't tell you how long it's been since I've had a date!"

"That's a little hard to believe," Sprenkel said. "You're very attractive. I'd think you'd have to fight men off with...." He suddenly thought better of this line of conversation and turned his attention to extracting them from their parking space. Around college campuses, he noticed, parking was always at a premium.

"With what?" Jill said.

"Come again?" He managed finally to get out of the space without doing major damage to the Corvette parked immediately behind him.

"I said, 'with what?'" Jill said. "What would I use to fend off the men you believe congregate outside my door? It's purely fiction, of course, but I enjoy a good metaphor as much as the next girl."

"Hard to believe," Sprenkel said again. "College men in Mississippi must be extra dense. Or blind. Is that it?"

"Not that I've noticed. But college students don't seem to date much, any more. They 'hook up.' Not the same thing at all."

"That's outside my experience," Sprenkel said.

"Oh, it's quite efficient. They just eliminate all that social folderol and go straight to the sex. It's cheaper, too. No expensive dinners or shows to deplete your wallet. You don't even have to change your sheets."

"I think I'm glad I missed all that," Sprenkel said.

"I know I am," she said.

They were on the bridge now, crossing into Louisiana. Below them, the Mississippi flowed implacably toward the Gulf of Mexico. Later, Jill remembered thinking that the river was unperturbed by the petty affairs of men—and women

Sprenkel seemed unimpressed by the river, staring neither to the left or right as he drove across the bridge. She wondered if he had simply seen it so many times that it no longer held a fascination for him, as it did for her. She had been in Natchez for two years, but she was still in thrall to this magnificent sight.

"I never get tired of seeing the Mississippi," she said, tentatively.

"I know what you mean," he said. "I've been here for five—going on six years now—and on my days off sometimes I just drive down to the levee and sit there watching it. Doesn't matter if there's traffic on the river; I'm happy just watching the current flow by, and the birds."

"Me, too," she said.

After a moment, she said: "Maybe we could stop now and do that for a while."

"That'd be nice, but I'm afraid we can't. Not right now. I'm on duty."

"On duty?" She tried, unsuccessfully, to keep the disappointment out of her voice.

"I'm sorry," he said, and he *did* sound apologetic. "I guess I misled you, although I didn't mean to. I asked you to go with me because I think I need your help. I'm trying to figure out who killed your roommate."

"I don't know what else I can tell you," she said. "I've told you everything I know."

"You saw that family photograph," he said. "As far as I can tell, you're the only person who *did* see it. You picked out her father from that photo of the corpse the other day."

"Yes, but…"

"I'm hoping," he said, "that you'll be able to identify your roommate's brother too, if we can find a photograph of him."

"Oh," she said.

They rode in silence for some time, both of them apparently immersed in their private thoughts. When they passed over the Old River dam, she began to have an inkling concerning their destination.

"Where are we going?" she asked.

"Morgan City," he said.

PLUM POINT, TENNESSEE

AUGUST 1829

By 1828, frustrated by the slow progress of clearing snags by hand, the government finally capitulated and authorized construction of a snag boat according to Shreve's specifications. Shreve named the boat *Heliopolis*.

The boat was built in Indiana, but low water prevented it from being pressed into service for several months. Finally, with the summer almost over, the river rose enough to permit the boat to leave the dock.

No one but Shreve seemed to hold much hope for this ungainly contrivance. For its first test, therefore, he had selected a section of the Mississippi where there were snags in abundance.

It was, everyone agreed, a strange-looking vessel. No one could recall ever before seeing a boat with *two* hulls. And the iron ram affixed to the twin hulls, below the waterline, was also a new wrinkle.

But the boat did exactly as Shreve had predicted. The iron ram grabbed the sunken trees and uprooted them. For trees that continued to resist the ram, an ingenious windlass and pulley system would yank them from the riverbed, where the onboard saw sliced them into manageable pieces, which the current would then carry downstream.

The snag boat made short work of the tangle, much to the amazement of the flotilla of boats, whose crews had come to watch and jeer. The taunts and catcalls died when the onlookers realized what they had seen. The taunts were replaced by shouts of joy.

Shreve heard the cheering but did not stop to bask in the glory. He sent the *Heliopolis* on downstream. There were other snags to remove all up and down the river.

MORGAN CITY, LOUISIANA

THE SIXTEENTH DAY

"Who is it that you want to see?" said the woman in the school office.

"I don't have a first name," Sprenkel said. "The last name would have been Van Dorn."

"I don't believe we have anyone by that name enrolled."

"Not now, I'm sure," Sprenkel said. "He would have been here in… maybe the late nineties."

"I'm sorry, but those records wouldn't be here anymore. After ten years or so, they go to storage."

"Surely they can be retrieved."

"Not easily, I'm afraid. Tell me again why you're seeking this information."

"All right," Sprenkel said, patiently. "This young man is the sole surviving member of his family. The others have all been killed—murdered, actually—and we have an obligation to notify him, as the next of kin. In fact, he seems to be the *only* next of kin."

"Oh, dear."

"Yes. You can see why this is so important."

"Yes. But before we go searching through old records, may I suggest an alternative? Would you recognize this young man from his high school photo?"

Sprenkel glanced at Jill.

"It's possible," he said.

"Then why don't you follow me to the school library? You can look through old yearbooks for his picture. It would make it easier to find him if we at least knew his first name."

As they followed the woman down the hallway, Jill whispered: "What if we don't recognize his picture?"

"We'll cross that bridge when we come to it," Sprenkel said.

They began their search with the 1999 yearbook and then worked backward. When they reached the beginning of the decade without seeing anyone they recognized, Sprenkel suggested that they look through more recent books. They began with the 2000 yearbook.

In 2002, they found him.

LOUISVILLE, KENTUCKY

1829

Another letter from Washington City awaited Shreve on his arrival at home. The powers that be had a new assignment for him. Shreve was unaccustomedly excited.

This was the big one: the Great Raft.

For centuries, the Red River had offered potential access to the new western lands, which the United States had purchased from France. But for centuries that potential had been denied. If a prospective settler wanted to reach the western lands, it was necessary to go overland. The river, long the primary and most efficient avenue of transportation in a country with few roads, was blocked by a massive logjam.

The logjam was known as the Great Raft. The first explorers sent by President Thomas Jefferson, after the Louisiana Purchase, discovered it when they attempted to navigate the river. It was said to extend more than a hundred and sixty miles, and it was so thick that in places, it was also said, a man could walk from one riverbank to the other without getting his feet wet. Bushes and grasses had taken root on the logs, and new trees had taken root as well. The log jam had become a virtual forest, not only covering the surface of the water, but extending—in many places—to the river bottom itself.

The origin of the Great Raft was unknown, but it was believed to have existed for more than five hundred years, long enough that Indians in the area had constructed myths to explain it. And the logjam was still growing. The river current had been reduced to less than one mile per hour, and the water impeded by this logjam had overflowed the river's banks. Enormous swamps had grown up on both sides.

It was not possible to go *through* the Great Raft. Commercial traffic, whether by steamboat or flatboat, was unthinkable. Jefferson's explorers had been forced to go around it—an arduous journey of several days through brackish bayous and muddy portages, where they were beset by insects, near-tropical heat, and disease. The first guide hired by the exploration party had, in fact, gotten lost.

River men had pleaded for years for the national government to step in and do something about the problem. Some half-hearted attempts had been made, but they had been abandoned as hopeless. Now, the superintendent of the western rivers, who had already accomplished so many difficult tasks, was being asked to deal with the biggest problem of all.

The task would require more than one snag boat and perhaps hundreds of men. It would require many months—perhaps years—but it would do more to encourage western expansion than anything else.

Shreve was excited. It was, at last, a job worthy of him, and he set to work immediately.

MORGAN CITY

THE SIXTEENTH DAY

"Here he is," Jill said. "I think."

Sprenkel had begun the library search looking over her shoulder, but he had found himself so distracted—by her beauty, her sweet disposition, her delicious *bouquet*—that he had forced himself to move away. He settled at a table at the far end of the room and pretended to study the latest *New Orleans Picayune*. This position offered the advantage of distance while not obstructing his view.

Now he hurried over to join her in peering at a senior class photograph of a blond teenager. Well, perhaps not blond; the black and white school photograph showed a youth with hair of a shade that might have been light brown. Below the hair was a Roman nose and thick lips. If he had been a girl, the lips might have been described as "bee stung."

"The book doesn't say his name is Van Dorn," Jill said. "And I haven't seen Harriet's family photograph for several months, but I'm almost positive that this is the face I remember."

The name under the picture was "Eddie Clinton."

"You're sure?" Sprenkel said.

"Almost. Like I said, it's been months since I saw the picture on her desk, but...."

"Keep looking a little longer," Sprenkel said. "Maybe you'll find another photo that looks even more like the man we're looking for."

"This is a high school photograph," Jill pointed out. "People do change as they get older. I know it hasn't been that long, but he might still have changed enough that I wouldn't recognize him."

"I know. But keep looking a little bit longer."

She nodded and turned back to the yearbooks.

Sprenkel studied the photograph. "Eddie Clinton," as he was identified in the yearbook, looked like a fairly typical high school senior, not at all what he had expected to find. But as he continued to look at the youthful face, he began to sense that he had seen the boy before. But not as a boy. As a man.

"I'm up to 2005," Jill said. "I haven't seen anyone else who looks familiar. Could I stop now?"

"Sure. The brother's got to be older than that, I'd think. Let's wrap it up. I'll see if I can persuade the office lady to chase down the file on Eddie Clinton."

"I really think he's the one," she said. "I really do. In spite of the difference in names."

"I think you're right," Sprenkel said. "But we'll see what else we can learn."

"Do you think we could go get some dinner first? I'm getting really hungry."

"I think that can be arranged," he said. "I'm hungry, too."

More than you can know, he thought to himself. *More than you can even imagine.*

NAGITOCHES, LOUISIANA

1829

His first sight of the Great Raft filled Shreve with dread. He had heard the stories; all river men had heard the stories, but this... morass... exceeded everything he had been told.

"Never seen anything like this," a bystander on the river bank said, shaking his head in wonder. "I come all the way up from New Orleans to see this. Now that I seen it, I still ain't sure I believe it."

"A hundred miles of this," Shreve said. "That's what I heard."

"Closer to two hundred, *I* heard," said his companion. "Hundred and fifty, easy. You sure you ain't bit off more than you can chew?"

"No," Shreve said, after a moment. "They're just snags. I've been clearing snags all up and down the Mississippi, the Ohio, the Illinois... We'll get these, too."

"There's snags, and then there's snags," said the bystander. "This one looks like them other snags' mama."

Shreve tended to agree but dared not say so.

"We'll get her," he said, after a moment.

I was right, he thought. *I'll need at least* two *snag boats, plus barges and boats to house the work crews. And I'll need to hire work crews! I'd better get busy on that.*

VIDALIA, LOUISIANA

THE SIXTEENTH DAY

"This is where you live?" Jill said. "In a *motel*?"

"It isn't a motel, any more," Sprenkel said. "The landlord converted all these units to apartments. It's got a kitchen with a dishwasher, and there's a back door, too."

She wrinkled her nose. "I guess it wouldn't be too bad, with the air conditioner running. It still *looks* like a motel, but…"

"It wouldn't be bad, I guess, *with* air conditioning. But it doesn't *have* air conditioning."

"None? At all?"

"No. I wish it did, but…"

"How can you live like this? In *Louisiana*!"

"Well, I'm not home, much. My job keeps me…"

"Without air conditioning, I wouldn't come home at all."

"Well, you know, people lived down here without air conditioning for centuries. They survived okay. I just imagine that it's 1860…"

It had been quite late when they returned from Morgan City, and Sprenkel had invited her to his apartment for a break before he drove her back across the river to Natchez. She had accepted with rather more eagerness than he had anticipated.

But now, her enthusiasm apparently had waned. Sprenkel wasn't surprised. He felt the same way about the apartment.

"That does it!" she said. "We're going to my place."

"I can't do that."

"Yes, you can. You know the way. It's just across the river, not ten miles from here. And *I* have air conditioning."

"But…"

"And you don't have to worry about me. I learned my lesson the last time. I won't hit on you again."

"All right," he said, finally. "Your place *would* be more comfortable. It's hard to have a decent conversation when you're sweating buckets."

"That's right."

"And we *do* need to talk. I guess I need to explain some things to you."

"Okay," she said. "We'll go to my place, and we'll talk. Just talk."

In the car again, Jill said, "So can you tell me whatever it is now, or should we wait until we get to my place?"

"I guess I can start," Sprenkel said. "It'll probably take a while."

"This is something really complicated?"

"Well, not complicated, exactly, but… I guess I *should* tell you now. That way, if you're completely disgusted with me by the time we get to your apartment, I can just drop you off, turn right around and head back across the river."

"That bad, huh?"

"Well, sort of, yeah. It's not something I'm proud of."

Jill waited expectantly, but Sprenkel seemed in no hurry to continue. The silence continued until they had crossed the river and they had pulled up in front of her apartment building. He switched off the engine and sat staring out the windshield, still silent.

Finally, she said, "I'm waiting."

After a moment he seemed to awaken from his reverie.

"Right. Okay. I've got to talk about it some time, I guess."

"It would probably be good for you to get it out."

"I doubt that," he said. "Still, I owe you."

She started to protest that he owed her nothing, but she caught herself in time. If Sprenkel felt obliged to tell her his story, who was she to interfere?

"I used to be married," he said, finally.

"Used to be?"

"We're divorced."

"Oh. I'm sorry."

"Yeah, me too. It's my own fault."

"Well," she said. "In cases like that, I think, there's usually plenty of blame to go around."

"Not in this case," Sprenkel said. "I had an affair."

Silence again.

"Oh," she said, after a moment. "What…"

"In Baltimore. We were both in uniform at the time, and we spent a lot of time together, the way you do in that kind of job. I thought she was hot. It just got harder and harder to keep my mind on the job."

"In my experience, limited as it is, an affair requires at least two people," Jill said. "Your partner must have had some involvement in this, too."

"Sure, but I don't think it meant as much to her as it did to me. I wasn't her first, and I suspect I wasn't her last."

Jill was silent, digesting this information.

"It was exciting while it lasted," Sprenkel said, after a moment. "We couldn't keep our hands off each other. We even did it once in the back seat of my squad car. Only once, though; I don't think my nerves could have handled that again. We were off duty, but I was late getting the car back to the lot."

"How did your employers learn about this?"

"That's just the thing. They never did. A lot of people knew, or suspected, but nobody turned us in."

"But something must have happened. You're not still involved with this woman, are you?"

"No, I'm not."

"Then what…"

"The *department* didn't hear about it," Sprenkel said. "But my wife did, and so did my partner's husband. Somebody told *them* about it. I don't know who. It doesn't really matter, any more."

"So your wife divorced you…"

"For infidelity. Actually, it wasn't much of a marriage by that time."

"And your partner?"

"Still married, as far as I know. Her husband forgave her, and they were trying to patch things up."

"Oh."

"Like I said, she was hot."

She shook her head in disgust.

"I'll never understand men. How can you go through life like that, in thrall to a pretty face?"

"You're kidding, right?"

"No, I am not. I cannot understand this preoccupation with physical beauty. An attractive woman appears in your field of vision, and you all turn to jelly. It's obscene. And ridiculous."

"May I respond?"

"Of course."

"My response is… George Clooney. Brad Pitt. Also Will Smith. Denzel Washington."

"Oh, right. The '*and you're another*' defense. I expected better from you than that."

"What can I say?" Sprenkel said. "You got me there. Guilty as charged, your honor. I throw myself on the mercy of the court—at least, I would if the court *had* any mercy."

"I'm only saying…"

"I know what you're saying," he broke in. "You've made it clear. I'm a heel, a cad, a philanderer, a breaker of marital vows. I admit it. I confess. All right?"

Silence.

"John," she said, finally. "I wasn't there; I can't know the circumstances, and after all it was... what... seven years ago?"

"No, you were right on the money. I'm pond scum."

"Come on, now. I didn't say..."

"Okay. You didn't say... whatever you didn't say. I'll walk you to your door. I wouldn't want you to be attacked by some *other* scumbag on your way inside."

"Not necessary," she said. "I'll take my chances, unless you'd like to come up with me?"

"I'd better get back," he said. "Got a long day tomorrow. I'll need my sleep if I'm going to be of any use. Got to be ready for whatever comes. You never know when I might see another pretty face."

"Well, then, I'll say good night."

"Good night."

She leaned over and a bestowed a brief, chaste kiss on his cheek.

"I enjoyed the day," she said. "In spite of everything."

Sprenkel did not reply. He waited until she had entered the building and then drove away silently, lost in thought. He spoke again only as he crossed the river alone.

"Damn!" he said. "Damn, damn, damn, damn, damn!"

Below him, the river still flowed silently and noncommittally to the gulf.

VIDALIA, LOUISIANA

THE SEVENTEENTH DAY

"Mr. Eastwood to see you, sir."

Sprenkel cursed under his breath. He didn't have time for a casual chat, which was all that Eastwood ever seemed to have in mind. He racked his brain, trying to dredge up a convenient excuse for avoiding the man. He came up with nothing.

"Send him in," he said.

The man who entered his office was clearly the same man Sprenkel had encountered previously, but he seemed profoundly changed. Where his previous visits had been casual in the extreme, Eastwood this morning was all bustle. He bounded into the room and stood imperiously at the desk, stern-faced and impatient.

"Sheriff, I need your help!"

"And a very good morning to you, too, Mr. Eastwood. How may I be of assistance?"

"Well, sir, you could begin by telling me about the Old River Control Structure."

"The Old River…" Sprenkel said, confused by the sudden introduction of an unexpected topic.

"Control Structure," Eastwood said. "Surely you've heard of it. It's in your jurisdiction."

"Not quite in my jurisdiction, but I know of it," Sprenkel said. "What is it that you'd like to know?"

"What is it and why is it there?"

"I'm not an expert on the subject," Sprenkel said. "There's a man on my staff who's rather more familiar with it. If you'd like, I can call him in. His name is…"

"I'm rather busy at the moment," Eastwood said. "Why don't you just tell me what *you* know about it?"

"All right. It's a dam with gates that control the flow of water from the Mississippi into the Atchafalaya. It was put in back in the 1950s…"

"And why was that done, sir?"

"Well, it was before my time here, you understand, but it's my impression that the structure was built to keep the Mississippi from changing course and taking over the Atchafalaya."

"And why was *that* done?"

Another strange conversation with the strange Mr. Eastwood!

"As I told you, it happened long before I came here," Sprenkel said. "I believe our Deputy Levesque could better answer your questions. I think he's in the office at the moment. It won't take a minute to call him…"

"I'm more interested in *your* understanding of the matter, Sheriff. Aren't you the man in charge here?"

"I suppose so," Sprenkel said. "However, my jurisdiction doesn't include the Old River Control Structure."

"Then whose jurisdiction is it?"

"I believe that honor goes to the Army Corps of Engineers. They're responsible for maintaining river navigation."

"Is that all?"

"Is *what* all?"

"Is river navigation the only matter you're concerned about?"

"I don't follow you."

"There are much more serious issues here, you know. Tampering with natural processes, for example. Who are we to try to alter the course that God has determined for it? Why are we attempting to overrule the laws of nature?"

Sprenkel shrugged.

"You're asking the wrong guy, I'm afraid," he said. "That's not my jurisdiction."

"But think of it, sheriff. If God has a plan for us, it would require tremendous hubris on our part to attempt to alter that plan, even for a good cause. Don't you agree?"

"That's not my area of expertise, either. Maybe a minister."

"Perhaps," said Eastwood. He didn't sound amenable. "In any event, there are serious policy questions involved here."

"Possibly, but I'm not in a position to deal with them. You probably need to talk to your congressman about that."

Eastwood shook his head. "I'm not rich. I can't make a big campaign contribution. I'm not even a registered voter. No reason in the world why some congressman would even bother with me. I depend on public servants to do their duty. That's why I'm talking to you."

"Well, you're talking to the wrong public servant," Sprenkel said. "I'm sorry, but there's nothing I can do for you, even if I understood what you want."

"You're the sheriff!"

"I work for the parish. Old River is federal property. You need to talk to the Corps of Engineers. I can give you a phone number, if you like."

"Thank you, but I can get the number for myself."

THE RED RIVER

1839

"That's the last of it," Shreve's foreman said. "No more logjams."

"For now," Shreve said. "We'll have to do this again in the not-too-distant future, though."

"Probably," the foreman said. "But it'll be somebody else's problem, next time."

The Great Raft was no more. Shreve felt a sense of accomplishment; he had completed a task that all before him had given up as impossible. The river was cleared of snags and obstacles all the way to the Mississippi. Commerce could now move on the river, which it had never been able to do before.

But the sense of accomplishment was tempered by the realization that it would all have to be done again. The river was not static; it was constantly changing in response to the weather, the seasons, the actions of mankind. There were already signs of incipient snag development—trees teetering on the riverbank.

Shreve had warned of this in his reports to the national government in Washington City. He feared, however, that his warnings would go unheeded. Having finally gone to considerable expense to open a vital transportation route, the government would not be eager to do it all again. Never mind that future projects would be far less difficult and expensive; he knew the reluctance was due to the principle of the thing as much as the expense.

Well, the principle *and* the expense.

VIDALIA, LOUISIANA

THE SEVENTEENTH DAY

After Eastwood left his office, Sprenkel went to the window and watched him drive away. He realized that he was still in the dark about the purpose of Eastwood's visit—or, for that matter, the purpose of *any* of his previous visits. How did Old River relate to pharmaceuticals, Eastwood's business?

If, indeed, pharmaceuticals *were* his business. Sprenkel realized that he had only Eastwood's assertion on that score. Now that he thought about it, Eastwood didn't strike him as a salesman at all. He made a note to himself to make some inquiries about Mr. Eastwood, as soon as he found the time to do so.

Whenever that might be, he thought ruefully. The murder investigation—problem-ridden as it was—was his first priority. He was making—had made—damned little progress on that matter.

On the other hand....

The thought brought him up short. He *knew* this man.

Rather, he knew *of* him, knew who he was. He had seen his face before, in a different context. But where had he seen it?

The folder containing his notes on the murder investigation should have been filed away by now, but it still sat on his desk. He had gotten into the habit of simply shoving it to an unused area of the desktop in order to deal with his day-to-day duties. He retrieved the file now and began leafing through it.

The file had grown quite large, and it took some time to go through it. He had no particular reason to spend much time on it, except that the investigation had been preying on his mind. It was a logical place to begin; the face of Mr. Eastwood might be in any one of the file drawers.

His instinct hadn't failed him. The face he was seeking *was* in this file. It was, to be sure, a much younger face, its subject having been in his late teens at the time the photo was taken, but the resemblance, Sprenkel thought, was unmistakable.

It was a photocopy of that page from the school yearbook in Morgan City. The face was the one Jill Winston had identified as the brother of her murdered flat mate.

What was the name? Not Eastwood, but Clinton. Eddie Clinton.

Clinton... Eastwood. It might be just the sort of alias that would occur to a man whose given name was the same as a well-known actor and film director: easy to remember, which would lessen the risk of forgetting it at a crucial time.

But Jill's flat mate was Harriet *Van Dorn*, not Clinton. Why would brother and sister have different names?

Actually, he realized when he thought about it, there were many reasons why siblings might have different surnames, adoption being one of them. Adopted children might not take their adoptive fathers' names. Foster children also might think of their foster parents as their own while retaining their own legal name. In fact, unless they were formally adopted, they probably couldn't legally change their surnames.

And of course, a man might also change his name in order to disguise his intentions, to make it more difficult for others to trace him. He couldn't imagine offhand, why Eastwood, or Clinton, would want to hide behind an alias.

Unless...

Unless he was secretly a murderer. And not merely a murderer but the murderer of his own sister. Sprenkel stopped himself from saying it aloud, but the thought was lodged in his consciousness now, and he knew it would not soon leave him.

What did he really know about this man? Virtually nothing, he realized. He lived in the parish, apparently, but he wasn't at home much, and his neighbors knew little about him. This information was actually second-hand, from Levesque, but Levesque was smart and diligent—a competent investigator. Sprenkel was inclined to trust Levesque's findings, as far as they went.

But how far was that? That was the question.

ST. LOUIS, MISSOURI

SEPTEMBER 1841

Two years had passed since Shreve's successful clearance of the Red River and his successful bypass of the meander at Turnbull's Bend. They were eventful years.

Martin Van Buren, who had succeeded Andrew Jackson as president, fell victim to a national financial meltdown (which he had not created) and was defeated for re-election. His successor, the Whig former governor of Indiana William Henry Harrison, died after only a month in office. The consensus of opinion was that he had caught pneumonia by going hatless on a cold, rainy inauguration day.

Harrison was succeeded by his vice president, John Tyler. Tyler was a Virginia aristocrat who had little interest in the west, or in the western rivers. Shreve's accomplishments, while appreciated, were not appreciated sufficiently to assure him of the "honor" of continuing as superintendent.

In mid-September, the hammer blow fell. A letter from Washington City informed Shreve that he was being replaced. He was instructed to turn over all the public property in his control to his successors. Since Shreve had never bothered to apply for patents, the "public property" included the snag boats that he had designed and invented—and used so successfully up and down the Mississippi and its tributaries.

He had purchased substantial acreage near St. Louis and had settled there to be near his flourishing steamboat business. And he had been thinking about the improvements he could introduce that would make his new land more profitable. He was a wealthy man by almost any measure and had no need to worry about his livelihood. But he needed a challenge, always a challenge.

Very well, he thought to himself. *I'll be a farmer.*

Shreve lived out his days as a farmer. He died before the great catastrophe befell the river. The American Civil War—the war that would virtually destroy the riverboat industry—was still nearly two decades away.

The first faint sounds of martial trumpets could already be heard, however, if a man knew how to listen.

PART 3

The history of man is a series of conspiracies to win from Nature some advantage without paying for it.

—Ralph Waldo Emerson, "Demonology"
Letters and Biographical Sketches, *1883*

VIDALIA, LOUISIANA

THE THIRD MONTH

"The thing is," Caulfield was saying, "After all this time I still don't have a handle on the son. Thanks for the heads-up on the father, though."

"Damn!" Sprenkel said, settling back in his chair. He tucked the phone on his shoulder and looked for the file on the murder. "I'd been meaning to call you about that! I got involved in, you know, everyday routine business, and I sort of put this thing on the back burner."

"I know how that can happen," Caulfield said. "What were you meaning to call me about?"

"I think I've maybe got a lead on the son, too. I haven't confirmed it, yet, but…"

"That's great!" Caulfield said. "This thing has been driving me crazy! I've been through all the Van Dorns in the metro area with no success. You have a new name?"

"Actually, I've got two or three names, but I think they're all the same guy. The last name is probably Clinton—Eddie or Edward, I think. Down here he's been going by the name Eastwood. He's using Clinton as his first name."

"Clinton Eastwood? Sounds like an alias, all right. You haven't found anybody named Van Dorn?"

"No Van Dorns so far. I don't think I'll find any, either. In fact, I've kind of been wondering if Van Dorn is a fake name, too. This whole family seems to be a work of fiction. Maybe they're a family of grifters."

"Wouldn't be surprised," Caulfield said. "Well, let's keep in touch."

After hanging up, Sprenkel sat at his desk, thinking. The idea hadn't occurred to him before, but it seemed to take on importance as he considered it now. Maybe "Van Dorn" *was* a fictitious name. Maybe the whole family *was* a fiction. Maybe the murder of Jill Winston's friend, the killing of "Angelo Sweet" in New Orleans, the slaughter of three people in Memphis, and the apparent disappearance of the son—maybe all these events were not the result of some outside event. Not gang warfare, no drug deal or series of drug deals gone bad—but rather the result of something else entirely, maybe some sort of gigantic scam gone wrong, or a family feud.

But a feud about what, precisely? And who were the two other victims of the massacre in Memphis—the man in the living room and the younger man in the back yard—who they had originally thought were members of the Van Dorn family? He had meant to ask Caulfield about them, but it had slipped his mind.

He called Caulfield back, but the detective had left his office. Sprenkel left word for him to return the call.

He sat, thinking, again—something he had not had much time to do recently. The image of "Clinton Eastwood" came to mind once more. Was he, in fact, the brother of Jill Winston's flat mate? And, if so, why was he operating under an alias? And why was he suddenly interested in Old River?

What did Old River have to do with the murder of Harriet Van Dorn? For that matter, was "Eastwood" even aware that his sister had been killed not far from that spot?

Perhaps, he thought, it was time to seek out Mr. Eastwood and ask him these questions directly.

MOUND CITY, ARKANSAS

APRIL 1865

Under normal circumstances, the loss of the steamboat *Sultana*, carrying Union soldiers and hundreds of former prisoners of war only recently released from the hell holes of Confederate prisons, would have been a major news story.

As it happened, however, the disaster was overshadowed by the events of a particularly eventful week. Earlier, Confederate General Robert E. Lee had gone shamefacedly to Appomattox Courthouse, Virginia, where he had signed the papers that surrendered his entire army to the army of Union General Ulysses Grant. Soon afterward, the actor John Wilkes Booth had taken his revenge on the north by assassinating President Abraham Lincoln. In context of the times, news of the *Sultana* disaster seemed much less important.

The Sultana had sailed originally with about 100 passengers and a crew of about 85. This was not an unusual passenger list; its legal capacity was 376 passengers, and it was common—in these late stages of the war—for the vessel to pick up many more people along her route under a contract with the government. Soldiers were being released from their duties and sent home; the *Sultana* was a convenient vehicle for this function.

At Vicksburg, the *Sultana* stopped for repairs to a leaking boiler. She was greeted by hordes of discharged soldiers, many of whom had spent much of the war in prison camps. They were tired, weak, and eager to return to their homes. Rather than replace the boiler—a three-day job—a patch was improvised so the boat could get under way after only a day.

But a one-day delay was more than enough time for the grim crowd of determined soldiers to bribe and force their way aboard the boat. The *Sultana* departed Vicksburg with more than 2,000 additional passengers, many in poor health, who spread out through the staterooms and hallways, and onto the outside deck. The boat labored feebly against the spring freshet under the additional weight.

Riverboats were not made to last forever. Before the advent of steam, most river men floated with the current downstream to New Orleans, sold their flatboats and keel boats there, and walked home rather than fight their way back upstream. Steam had made it possible to sail against the current, but even these new craft were not expected to serve more than a few years. They were built of wood, like their predecessors, and the onboard presence of large, high-pressure steam engines made them much more vulnerable to fire.

Henry Miller Shreve, if he had still lived, could have told them about fire.

The *Sultana* labored sluggishly onward, past Memphis, and, as she approached the mouth of the Ohio River, the boiler finally gave way. The explosion of one boiler caused a chain reaction, and three of the boat's four boilers were eventually destroyed.

Sparks from hot coals showered the crowded deck. The force of the explosions blew many passengers into the river. Fire broke out throughout the vessel, and the agonized cries of the injured and dying could be heard on shore. The boat drifted helplessly downstream.

The explosion occurred at about 2:00 am. The first boat on the scene did not arrive for another hour. By that time, the carnage was catastrophic. Many passengers who did not die in the explosion and fire, died from exposure and hypothermia in the cold water of the Mississippi.

Among those Americans who learned of the *Sultana* disaster, sabotage was commonly suspected. Indeed, Confederate sympathizers had long seen the writing on the wall and had been busily scuttling riverboats—to keep them out of Union hands. A government investigation, however, concluded that the *Sultana* was the victim of hasty and careless maintenance—and nothing more.

In any event, the era of passenger travel on the rivers had passed. Americans had discovered the railroads, which could carry a man to his destination faster and cheaper.

Freight, of course, was a different matter. For cargoes that were not subject to time constraints—grain and coal, among others—the rivers were still popular.

FERRIDAY, LOUISIANA

THE THIRD MONTH

"Nobody here by that name," the woman at the door said, with finality.

"Maybe he isn't going by Eastwood," Sprenkel said. "How about Van Dorn?" It was hot in the sun, and his patience was wearing thin.

"Nobody by that name, either," said the woman, and made to shut the door.

"I don't understand," Sprenkel said. "When did he move?"

"Never."

"Never?"

"This ain't no boarding house," she said. "Don't take in roomers. Never done that, and I been living here near twenty years."

"One of the neighbors, maybe? You see a white guy walking around in the neighborhood, somebody you didn't know?"

"*What* neighborhood?"

"I asked you first."

"And *I* askin' *you*. What neighborhood? You see any neighborhood here? 'Nother house about a half mile that way, one more 'bout two miles other way. This look like a *neighborhood* to you?"

"No," Sprenkel said. "I guess it doesn't. Sorry to bother you, ma'am."

As he turned away, he heard the door slam behind him. The woman seemed to put a little extra force into the action, as if warning him not to bother her again.

"Damn!" he said, aloud. For a moment he stood by the roadside and tried to think.

Now where do I go? And what do I do?

THE LOWER MISSISSIPPI RIVER

1927

Control of the Mississippi River in flood time had long been the subject of debate. There were two basic schools of thought on the matter. One school argued that levees—those great earthen dikes that held the river channel in check—were the only reliable and affordable method of preventing a disastrous flood on the lower river. The other faction argued that levees alone would never be adequate in themselves; that the river needed other outlets along the way—lakes and swamps and reservoirs—to absorb some of the excess water.

Most people preferred solution number one. Creating outlets, it was thought, would eat up valuable farmland and slow the current of the river. As the river slowed, its ability to carry away sediment would diminish; consequently the level of the river would rise, and the likelihood of flooding would actually increase.

The test of these theories occurred early in the twentieth century.

In the late summer of 1926, rain began to fall in torrents throughout the upper Midwest. Farmers, who paid attention to such things, were astonished not only by the magnitude of the rainfall, but by the event itself. The months of July through September were usually the dry season, and prolonged rain at this time of year was unusual in the prairie states. Flooding was even more unusual; in the dry season, the parched ground was capable of absorbing prodigious amounts of water.

But in 1926 and 1927, one storm followed another in quick succession. Soon every major river in the Mississippi watershed had spilled onto the surrounding flood plains: the Illinois, the Floyd River, the Sioux River, the Wabash, the Tennessee, the Cumberland. Some Midwestern states received more rain in three days than they had normally received in three months.

In January of the following year, the Monongahela and Allegheny Rivers also overflowed their banks and inundated the city of Pittsburgh. A few days later, the Ohio River flooded downtown Cincinnati.

Livestock drowned, crops were destroyed, people were forced from their homes, and still the rains came. The riverbeds, which typically served as sponges soaking up the summer rainfall, reached saturation points and became, instead, conduits that funneled the flood downstream. Even the Arkansas River, a wide but shallow stream that Mark Twain had once said would be easier to pave than to make navigable, overflowed its banks and swamped the city of Little Rock. And Little Rock was more than one hundred miles upstream from the Mississippi.

The rain began to let up by mid-October, 1927, and the people who lived upstream heaved a sigh of relief. But downstream, at Natchez and Baton Rouge and New Orleans to the south, the trouble was only beginning. All that water was on its way to the Gulf of Mexico, and these cities were in the way.

The flood hit Louisiana and Mississippi like a hammer. The damage that had been inflicted on people upstream was compounded here by the sheer volume of water and silt that the river brought with it from the north, and by the high levees that had been built to prevent the lower river from spilling over into populated areas.

The levees had the further effect of channeling the river, thereby increasing its velocity, which in turn increased the force of the water. The levees had been saturated and weakened by months of nearly constant rainfall. They began to develop leaks, which local people called "crevasses." Water poured through the crevasses, destroying even more cropland, livestock, farms—and people.

To alleviate the danger downstream, officials agreed to open additional crevasses in the levees upstream. These actions relieved some of the threat to New Orleans, even while inundating more upstream villages and farms.

It was a national emergency, calling for the intervention of the federal government. President Calvin Coolidge declined to visit the disaster area, but Secretary of Commerce Herbert Hoover came in his stead. Hoover's intensive involvement in the relief effort gained him a national reputation that contributed to his victory in the next presidential election.

By the time the flood of 1927 receded, in April, it was estimated that more than 75,000 people had been forced from their homes. An untold number had died.

In the wake of the great flood, officials from Washington and from the river basin huddled in solemn assemblies and concluded that too many levees had failed.

Obviously, the solution was to build the levees higher.

VIDALIA, LOUISIANA

THE THIRD MONTH AND ONE DAY

"I'm sorry about that," Levesque said. "I shoulda confirmed that our guy actually lived where he said he lived. I dropped the ball."

"It didn't seem all that important at the time, I guess," Sprenkel said. "But it's started me wondering, again. The guy's got to live somewhere. Why's he making it so hard to find him? He must know we'll find him eventually, if we really need to."

"Maybe he doesn't care about 'eventually,'" Levesque said. "Maybe he's just concerned about right now."

"I don't follow you."

"Maybe," Levesque said, "he figures that it won't matter if we find him *eventually*. If he's got something planned, and he can pull it off, he can disappear for good once it's done."

Sprenkel considered this. "That would mean that he's planning something big, and probably illegal."

"Probably."

"And not just illegal. Catastrophic, maybe."

"Right. What do you suppose?"

"I don't know," Sprenkel said. "The first time we talked, he was asking about fishing spots. I couldn't help there."

"And this time?"

"He asked me about Old River. He wanted to know what it was there for, and why. I tried to direct him to you…"

"Thanks a lot."

"You're welcome. But apparently he just wanted to talk to me, to rant, it seemed like. All about fooling around with nature, preventing the river from doing what it wants to do. That sort of thing."

"Some kind of religious argument?"

"I guess, yeah."

"I sure am glad," Levesque said, "that he didn't want to talk to me. That's way outside my expertise."

TURNBULL'S BEND

SPRING 1950

It was probably a farmer who first noticed that something was happening to the river. Walking his fields in the early spring, he would have climbed a levee and realized, after a time, that the river was changing its course. The spring floods were rushing toward the Gulf of Mexico, as always, but much of the flood was going west, toward the Atchafalaya River, rather than south toward New Orleans.

More than a century before, Henry Miller Shreve had created a shortcut to eliminate a long, swooping bend in the river, Turnbull's Bend, which had forced river traffic to go many miles out of the way. By digging a new channel across a spur of land, Shreve cut off Turnbull's Bend and shortened the trip.

But this new shortcut also connected with the Red River, a tributary of the Mississippi. A portion of the Red River ran parallel and in close proximity to a portion of the Atchafalaya River. The Atchafalaya, which emptied into the gulf west of New Orleans at Morgan City, took a shorter and steeper course to the sea.

By clearing the Red River logjam known as the Great Raft, Shreve had made the Red viable for river traffic. But clearing the Great Raft had also increased the flow of water on the Red River, and this new flood sought new outlets to the sea. Some of the overflow continued on to the Mississippi, but much of it found its way to the Atchafalaya.

As a result, the Red River became primarily a tributary of the Atchafalaya, rather than the Mississippi. By creating his shortcut, Shreve had made it inevitable that the Mississippi would also change its course and become, essentially, a tributary of the Atchafalaya. On its new course, the river would bypass New Orleans, Baton Rouge, and everything in between.

Engineers for the United States Army, who had been given the responsibility for maintaining river navigation, concluded that this was a major problem. Left unchecked, the Atchafalaya would capture more and more of the Mississippi. Over time it would, in fact, *become* the

Mississippi. The present river channel would become merely a tidal estuary.

And what would this development mean for New Orleans and Baton Rouge, the two major cities situated below the Atchafalaya? The 130-mile stretch of river between the two cities was crowded with industrial sites that depended on the river for their outlet to the sea. The Port of New Orleans had become one of the largest, and busiest, in the nation.

Some river traffic might still be able to use some portion of the old route. Some, but not all.

And for the million or so people who lived in those cities below the Atchafalaya, this outcome would be a disaster. The Mississippi River was the source of drinking water for both cities. The brackish water of a tidal estuary would not be potable, and without drinking water those people would be doomed.

Nearly everyone agreed that this was an untenable situation; something had to be done. And the Old River Control Structure was born.

VIDALIA, LOUISIANA

THE THIRD MONTH AND THREE DAYS

The voice on the phone was familiar, even though Sprenkel had not heard it in months.

"John... Sheriff?"

"Good morning, Jill. I'm happy to hear from you."

"Oh, I doubt that," she said.

"You doubt it?"

"I haven't heard from you in months, after all."

"I'm sorry about that," Sprenkel said, shamefaced. "I'm afraid I didn't think you'd want to hear from me, after..."

"After that night, you mean."

"Well, yeah."

A moment of silence.

"I'll admit, it *did* give me something to think about," she said. "And I *did* think about it."

"And?"

"And... I guess... I'm still thinking about it. But that isn't why I called... exactly. I was just wondering if you could tell me anything more about the murder investigation. About Harriet."

Should I tell her? What's the harm?

"Well, I think I've found your roommate's brother," he said.

"Really? Did he know about Harriet's death?"

"I don't know," Sprenkel said. "I wasn't sure it was him until yesterday, and when I went looking for him again, I couldn't find him."

"Oh," she said. "Well, what did you think of him? What's he like?"

"He's a bit strange."

"Strange?"

"I can't quite figure him out," Sprenkel said. "He talks in religious language, but he uses it in different ways. Most of the folks around here talk about sin and redemption, and heaven and hell. This guy talks about God a lot, but he doesn't mention sin, or hell. He... I don't know... he talks about God and nature and... I sure would like to find someone who could straighten all this stuff out. I think I need a guide, or a road map, or something."

"Actually," she said, after a moment, "I might know just the man to talk to about that."

NATCHEZ, MISSISSIPPI

THE THIRD MONTH AND FOUR DAYS

"I appreciate your taking the time to see me," Sprenkel said. "I realize this is rather short notice."

"Not a problem," said the Reverend Herbert Jasparow. "Ms. Winston has been to see me before, and spoken to me about some serious issues. I'm assuming your inquiry is concerned with the same matter?"

"In a manner of speaking, yes," Sprenkel said. "I'm investigating a murder, but our investigation has taken us in… rather a strange direction. I have no expertise in this area, so Jill… Miss Winston… suggested that I talk to you."

"Interesting," Jasparow said. "If I can help you, I'll be happy to do so. I take it this is concerned with religion in some way?"

"That's right. More specifically, it's religious *language* I'm interested in."

Jasparow leaned back in his desk chair. "I'm listening," he said, with an expansive gesture.

"It's a little difficult for me to explain," Sprenkel said. "But I've dealt a couple of times now with a man that I think is up to something."

"Something evil?"

"Maybe. Probably something illegal, at least. At any rate, he's been using religious terminology in ways that I don't understand."

"What sort of terminology?"

"I think I'm more concerned about the terminology he *isn't* using. He doesn't talk about sin, for example. Every religious person I've dealt with talks a lot about sin. This guy talks about God like God is a business man who wants to sue us for breach of contract."

Jasparow nodded.

"Covenant theology," he said.

"What's that?"

"In the Old Testament," Jasparow said, "God makes a covenant with Israel. Sort of a contract: 'You worship me, follow my rules, and I'll take care of you.' I've simplified it a bit, but that's the essence of it."

"And this... contract. Is it still in effect?"

"Depends on who you ask, I suppose. I think most Christians believe they still have a relationship with God that sounds a lot like a contract."

"How would God, say, enforce a contract like that?" Jill asked.

"Depends on who you ask, again. Disease, pestilence, fires, floods. Just about any disaster could be attributed to violations of the covenant. A lot of people believe that sort of thing."

"Do you?" she asked. "Do you believe that God is punishing us for our... what, sins?"

"I don't know."

"That sounds as if you *do* believe that sort of nonsense," she said.

"I don't know. I've had enough science courses to know the reasons why most of these disasters occur, but that doesn't mean God isn't behind them. Or that he *is*, for that matter. The Old Testament prophets made that argument a lot."

"I've read a lot of that prophetic literature," Jill said. "They sound crazy to me."

"It's possible," Jasparow said, "to be both crazy—and *right.*"

BATON ROUGE, LOUISIANA

THE THIRD MONTH AND FIVE DAYS

It serves me right for majoring in English.

Jill had never before questioned her choice of a field of study, but she had come to regret not having studied computer science, or at least, having signed up for one of the ubiquitous courses in navigating the Internet, which had seemed to proliferate on campus recently. She had always thought, rather smugly it seemed now, that she had chosen a subject that would be impervious to the allure of life online. She had always assumed that she would be able to exist quite happily among her treasured books—avoiding the barbaric dictatorship of cyberspace. What need would she have for the Internet, aside from an occasional foray into those few professional journals that only existed online? It was true that their numbers were growing—exponentially—as the cost of paper and ink mushroomed, but she had felt certain that the need for "dead tree literature" would remain.

But now....

Now, it seemed that the very structure of everyday life had been cruelly altered to require an online existence. A simple inquiry into state government records, although theoretically possible, required an online presence. An understanding of Internet protocols—an understanding borne of intimate knowledge and experience of the inner workings of the cyber world. Which she did not possess.

And so she found herself deeply involved in the pursuit of state corporate records, seeking information about the officers and directors of the Madeleine Corporation. She knew the name of its principal—Roger Van Dorn—but other names were not forthcoming, except by paying a fee to the state. And that she could not—would not—permit herself to do.

It happened that it was a relatively simple undertaking, and she cursed herself for her intransigence. But now she had the information, and she sped north to pass along the information to John Sprenkel.

Perhaps he could determine what it all meant. She had an idea, but she would wait eagerly for his interpretation.

VIDALIA, LOUISIANA

THE THIRD MONTH AND FIVE DAYS

"I understand you've been looking for me," said the Man of God.

"That's right," Sprenkel said. "And you've been a rather difficult man to find, Mr. Eastwood."

"I think we can dispense with the subterfuge by now, don't you?" the Man of God said. "You probably know me as Edward Clinton, by now. You can just call me Eddie, or Edward, which would actually be my preference."

The man had been waiting when Sprenkel arrived that morning. Rather than waiting inside the office, he had stood beside his car and nodded to the sheriff as he drove up. Sprenkel pulled in behind the car, prepared to follow the man if necessary. It had not been necessary.

"Actually, I know you by several names," Sprenkel said. "How do you feel about Edward Van Dorn?"

"I'm afraid that's a name to which I do not respond well," the Man of God said. "Too many unpleasant memories, I fear, are related to that name."

"But you are, are you not, the brother of Harriet Van Dorn?"

"Legally, I suppose, since Roger Van Dorn adopted us both."

"Legally?"

"As opposed to morally. It was not in any sense a familial relationship. Roger was not a father to us in any meaningful way. Not to either of us, nor a husband to his wife."

"How would you describe that relationship, then?"

"To me," Clinton said, "he was a taskmaster. A petty tyrant. A pettifogging lawyer."

"And to Harriet?"

"Ah, their relationship was much simpler."

"Which was…"

"A very simple relationship, indeed. He was her pimp.

"I've no problems with adoption, in itself," Eastwood—or Clinton—continued. "Adoptive parents usually have some affection for the children they take into their families, or so I've been told."

"But not in your case?"

"Nothing of the sort. We were the means to an end. Sources of revenue. He whored out Harriet—his wife, as well—and kept most of their earnings."

"Did he do that with you, as well?"

Eastwood/Clinton frowned and shook his head.

"I believe he would have done so, if he had thought if feasible. I'm sure he considered it, but the market simply wasn't there. He tried me himself, but I suspect he found me insufficiently enthusiastic."

"But Harriet *was* enthusiastic?"

"Not at first, but I think she grew to enjoy it. Perhaps 'enjoy' is too strong a word, now that I think of it. I suspect that she enjoyed the approval she received from Van Dorn. He could be quite charming, if he chose to be."

Sprenkel considered this new information and decided that it made sense, to a degree. But it left several questions unanswered.

"Did you kill your sister?" he asked, after a moment.

"No, I did not," Clinton/Eastwood replied. "But I was present when it happened."

* * * *

Ohmigod! John was right! That's Harriet's brother!

Jill recognized the man immediately, even from the distance of nearly half a block. The man to whom Sprenkel was speaking was unmistakably the brother in Harriet's family photograph, even though she had not seen it in months. The photograph which had disappeared when Harriet had disappeared... Perhaps the brother had removed it in order to confuse those who might make the connection between them.

The connection she had made.

Jill sat in her car watching as Sprenkel chatted with the man. They were speaking amiably enough, she thought, although she sensed an undercurrent of tension between the two. Not surprising under the circumstances, considering the difficulties Sprenkel had encountered in his attempt to locate Harriet's brother. The brother's efforts to lead him astray must have been frustrating, as well.

She wanted to rush forward and confront the brother with her new information, but she decided to wait. The information might be useless now—or at least unimportant—and in any event might be more valuable to Sprenkel if she were not to spill it in the brother's presence.

So it was decided. She would wait and inform Sprenkel in private. That would be the wiser choice.

* * * *

"So you've heard about my skeeter? I've been wanting to tell someone about it for a long... well, for several months, now," Clinton said.

They were on their way to Ferriday. Clinton was driving, with Sprenkel in the front passenger seat. Clinton had been prepared to use force, if it had been necessary, but Sprenkel had readily agreed to go with him.

"Your skeeter?"

"That's just my name for it," Clinton said. "It looks a little like a mosquito, only bigger, of course. You'll see."

Clinton turned into a short driveway beside a yellow, wood-frame farmhouse and shut off the ignition. He sat quietly for a moment, while Sprenkel listened to the sound of metal contracting in Clinton's cooling engine.

"I bought it about a year ago and put it together by myself," Clinton said, and Sprenkel could hear the enthusiasm in his voice. "I'd heard about ultralights for a while, and it sounded like fun. It was a little harder to build than I'd expected, but it *is* fun to fly. The best part is that it's easy to keep up, and I don't need a pilot's license."

"Use a lot of gas?"

"Not so much. It's just a little two-cycle engine—kind of like a lawn-mower—so repairs are fairly simple, too. Come on, and I'll show you."

Clinton lifted the bar on the door to a barn behind the farmhouse. He swung the door open, revealing a building empty of everything but something covered by a tarpaulin. He lifted the covering gently to reveal a miniature helicopter.

"And it actually flies?" Sprenkel said. "Hard to believe."

"Oh, it flies—quite well, in fact," Clinton said. "It's not real fast, and it won't get a lot of height, but it's a lot of fun. A real adventure."

"Can you carry passengers?" An idea had been forming in Sprenkel's mind: this could have been the instrument of Harriet Van Dorn's death.

"Well, it's no 747," Clinton said. "There's room for just me and one passenger, if the passenger isn't too heavy."

"Like your sister."

"You figured that out, I guess. Yes, I took her up, but I didn't push her out. One minute she was there, and the next minute she wasn't. "

"She jumped? Suicide?

"I believe so. I had been telling her about our... father. Laying out the truth for her. I suppose it was more than she wanted to hear. I feel bad about it."

I should hope so, Sprenkel thought, but Clinton didn't sound as if he felt bad about it.

"The sudden loss of her weight unbalanced me," Clinton continued. "It took me a few minutes to regain control, and by that time I was quite some distance away."

"Did you look for her?"

"Of course! It took me nearly an hour in the dark, and when I found her she was beyond help."

"Still, you could have called for assistance."

"Well, it was a bit of a sticky situation. I shouldn't have had a passenger with me at all—you *do* need a pilot's license for that—so I knew I'd be in for real trouble if I reported it. I just figured someone would find her and call it in to the authorities, and I was right. After all, you found her."

"Someone called it in. It should have been you."

Clinton shrugged. "Water over the dam, now. No harm done. Want to go up for a ride?"

"You just told me you're not licensed to carry passengers," Sprenkel pointed out. "You'd have your little aircraft confiscated, and you'd probably get a fine."

"Someone would have to report me, first," Clinton said. "You wouldn't do that, would you?"

"I'm a sworn police officer," Sprenkel said. "I took an oath to enforce the law."

He leaned over to inspect the little craft closely. "It's really a neat little contraption, though. I'll have to say that…"

He felt the hard pressure of a gun barrel pressing against his back. *His* gun! Sprenkel cursed himself silently for dropping his guard.

"Actually," Clinton said, "I'm afraid I must insist on that ride."

"I can't do that," Sprenkel said. "I can't put myself in the position of breaking…"

He didn't finish the sentence. A searing pain rushed through his head as the butt of his gun crashed at the base of his skull. Darkness followed.

FERRIDAY, LOUISIANA

ONE HOUR LATER

Was it a blue car? Or a black car?

Jill wished she could remember more about the car in which Harriet's brother had driven away, with John Sprenkel accompanying him. This was a bit strange, she thought. Sprenkel's car was parked immediately behind the brother's car. Why hadn't Sprenkel simply followed in his own vehicle?

For the present, she had a more serious problem. She had lost sight of the car as it sped away, and she had been trying for more than an hour to catch up with it. The problem was compounded by her realization that she had not paid close enough attention to the vehicle itself. It was a dark-color, late-model sedan, she knew, but so many cars looked alike.

She drove as fast as she dared; fortunately there was little traffic on the road. Her target had been heading north, out of town. Soon she found herself in another community—the sign said "Ferriday"—and she had not reacquired the target.

She passed through the community and into the rural countryside beyond it. The houses—never too densely settled to begin with—had thinned out again, and were situated far from the road. She lowered her speed and peered carefully at each driveway, looking for her quarry and hoping that she would recognize it if she saw it.

The most likely possibility was parked beside a yellow farmhouse, which sat about fifty yards back from the road. It looked like the right car, but she couldn't be certain. She drove on a little way past the house, parked in an out-of-sight location, and began walking back. She wished she had brought binoculars with her—it would have enabled her to stay farther away—but she had come empty handed. There was nothing she could do but approach the house as stealthily as possible, and wait.

She did not have to wait long. The door to the barn behind the house opened, and a man appeared. She thought he looked like the brother, although she couldn't be certain from her distant observation post. The man was towing something attached to a rope. The object appeared to be a machine of some kind.

A small helicopter, perhaps, she thought. Strange.

The brother—if it was the brother—returned to the barn and soon emerged with a man in tow—a man whom she recognized as Sprenkel. Well, perhaps "in tow" wasn't the proper description; the sheriff seemed to be helped along, as if Sprenkel were... what... drunk? Ill? Could he have had a heart attack?

As she watched, the man set Sprenkel (she was sure, now) on the contraption's rear seat and set about securing him. The process seemed to involve the use of some sort of binding—bungee cords? No, it was on a roll. Duct tape? Whatever it was took several minutes.

When he had completed this chore, the man proceeded to unfold the rotor blades, which were attached to a central mast. Then the man seated himself on the craft and began fooling with something at his feet. The contraption roared into life; it sounded like a lawnmower.

Startled by the sound, she retreated to the relative safety of her car. As she continued watching, the contraption began slowly rising into the air. As she watched, dumbfounded, the little craft rose to a height of several hundred feet before veering off in a southerly direction.

She had never seen such a craft before, but as it passed overhead she confirmed two things: the man flying it was Harriet's brother, and the man riding slumped over behind him was Sheriff John Sprenkel.

VIDALIA, LOUISIANA

THIRTY MINUTES LATER

Levesque received the call in his car, patched through by the dispatcher. The call was from Jill Winston, and she was frantic. She had to repeat herself a couple of times before Levesque could understand the gist of her message.

"You're sure it was Sprenkel in this helicopter thing?" he said.

"Absolutely. And I don't think he was conscious, or at least he was dazed, maybe injured."

"Where are you now?" he asked.

"I'm on my way back from Ferriday. I'm probably about ten minutes away."

"All right," Levesque said. "I'm in my car. I'll meet you at the bridge."

In a few minutes, he saw her car approaching. He got out of his vehicle and signaled to her. She pulled in behind him.

"Get in," he said. "Your car will be okay here, and we can make better time if you come with me."

"I don't have any idea where they were going," she said, breathlessly, as she slipped into the passenger seat.

"I've got an idea," he said. "We found a place that I think he's been using. It's not too far away, but it's in Mississippi."

"Mississippi?" Jill said. "But what…"

"Hang on," Levesque said, and he stepped on the accelerator.

THE ABANDONED AIRSTRIP, RURAL MISSISSIPPI

THAT EVENING

Pain and nausea. And darkness.

Sprenkel understood the pain, the result of a hit from a gun butt at the base of his skull. And the nausea was the natural result of the excruciating pain. The darkness, however… Had he gone blind?

It occurred to Sprenkel, after a moment, that the darkness was probably due to the duct tape that Clinton had applied over his eyes. And not only his face: his upper body had been tightly wrapped with tape to immobilize his arms and hands. The attack had not only knocked him unconscious, he thought ruefully. It had made him stupid

He had little experience with duct tape, but apparently it was much stronger than he had imagined.

His legs, strangely enough, had not been bound. He tried to stand and found that he could not. Dizzy, in pain, and blindfolded, he could not regain his balance. He fell painfully to the floor.

"I suppose I should have warned you about that," Clinton said. "You shouldn't try to get up if you can't see what you're doing."

"So you're here," Sprenkel said. "I didn't hear you so I thought…"

"You thought you were alone. I know. Sorry to have misled you."

"When are you going to let me go? You can't keep me like this forever."

"I don't know yet. I'll let you know when I do."

Sprenkel heard him moving around somewhere behind him. Clinton seemed to be moving something—several somethings—outside. He left and returned several times.

"What are you doing?" Sprenkel asked when the man returned.

"Nothing you need to worry about," Clinton replied. "You aren't going anywhere—not for a while, anyway."

"You're going to leave me here?"

"For a while. You'll be okay. The lions and tigers are outside and can't get to you."

"Lions and tigers? In Mississippi?"

"Well, bears, then." He chuckled. "You're still safe in here."

He heard Clinton go out. It was difficult, with his hands and arms immobilized, but he set to work attempting to move the duct-tape blindfold, rubbing his head on his shoulder in the hope of dislodging the covering. He had made some progress, but the head movement caused his nausea to return. He vomited, and much of the vomit landed on his chest.

He heard his captor laughing somewhere behind him.

"Oh, look at you now," Clinton said. "You've made such a mess. I just can't take you anywhere."

"If you took me home, I could clean myself up," Sprenkel said, but Clinton had apparently already left the room.

THE ABANDONED AIRSTRIP, RURAL MISSISSIPPI

That Evening

"What a dismal place," Jill said.

"You should have seen it before," Levesque said. "Somebody's been in here with a weed whacker recently. This old road was practically overgrown, last time we were in here."

"Hard to believe."

"Take my word for it," Levesque said. He stopped the car and switched off the ignition.

"I think we're far enough away that he won't see the car," he said. "It's a chance we'll have to take. There's no place to hide it at the airstrip."

"Do you think he's there?"

"If he isn't, he will *be* there. Either that or he just left."

"If he's gone already, how will we know his plans?"

"I think I know his plans already, but I'd prefer to catch him before he puts his plans in motion."

"And *before* he decides to kill the sheriff!" Jill said, with a touch of panic.

"I don't think that's part of his plan. Not his original plan, at least."

As they approached the air strip, Levesque found new rubber markings on the strip that indicated the ultralight had been there quite recently.

"That's it, then," he said. "Maybe we can beat them to their destination, though."

"Where is that?"

"Eastwood, or whatever his name is, is heading for Old River. I'd bet on it."

"I wonder," Jill said as they began returning to the car. "Do you think we should look around in that old building over there?

"The sheriff and I checked it out when we were here before, but that was a few months ago," Levesque said unenthusiastically. "I guess it can't hurt to check it out again, if we're quick about it."

They were mildly surprised to find that the front door to the little shack was unlocked. They were rather more surprised to find Sprenkel inside, still wrapped in duct tape.

ON THE ROAD TO OLD RIVER

HALF-AN-HOUR LATER

"I'm a little surprised he left you behind," Levesque was saying as he barreled along the road toward Old River.

"I don't think he had a choice. I heard him making several trips out to his little 'skeeter,' as he calls it. He was loading something onboard, and he needed to unload any excess weight. Otherwise, he might not have been able to take off."

"Interesting. What do you suppose he's carrying?"

"If I had to guess," Sprenkel said. "I'd say it was C4."

Levesque emitted a low whistle.

"So he's really serious about this," he said. "I have to admit, I've had my doubts."

"I did, too." Sprenkel said. "Right up until the point when I woke up with a splitting headache and taped to that chair."

"What is C4?" Jill asked.

"It's a high explosive," Levesque said. "They used a lot of it in Vietnam."

"What does he plan to use it for?

"He wants to blow up Old River," Sprenkel said. "He's got this hangup about people tinkering with the natural order of things."

"He wouldn't have to blow it up entirely," Levesque added. "If he causes enough damage, the river will do the rest."

"They could repair it, though, couldn't they?" Jill said.

"They could," Sprenkel said. "But *would* they? Remember Hurricane Katrina and all the damage it caused? There was a lot sentiment in Congress that it would be too expensive to repair the damage. A lot of people just wanted to forget the whole thing."

"Really? After all those people died?"

"They're not a factor. Dead people don't vote," Levesque said.

"There he is!" Sprenkel said.

He pointed to a field along the road. Clinton had landed his ultralight and was busily engaged in shifting his cargo.

"Looks like he's having problems with the C4, if that's what it is," Levesque said. "I'd guess it's moving around and throwing him off-balance."

"Let's see if we can give him a hand," Sprenkel said. "Pull over here; we'll need to move fast."

Levesque did so. He and Sprenkel sprinted across the field, leaving Jill with the car.

"Be careful," Sprenkel said. "He's got a gun."

"He's got *your* gun," Levesque said. "And I'm guessing he knows how to use it."

Clinton heard them coming and rushed back to his cockpit in an attempt to get airborne before they arrived. Sprenkel recognized the sound of the little engine starting up, and he found an additional burst of energy to move him across the remaining distance.

The little aircraft began rising. With a sinking feeling in his gut, Sprenkel lunged for the craft and managed to grab the undercarriage just as Levesque arrived behind him.

"He's getting away! Grab onto something!" Sprenkel shouted. Levesque managed to get hold of a landing skid on the opposite side of the aircraft. The helicopter swung wildly for a second before Clinton managed to right it again.

The ultralight continued to rise, but the added weight caused its ascent to slow significantly. Sprenkel heard the strain on its capacities as its tiny engine fought for altitude.

Sprenkel began desperately swinging his body in the hope of creating greater instability. The gambit seemed to have some small success; the little aircraft began swinging to counterbalance the effects of his body mass.

"You trying to kill us?" Levesque shouted. "You see how high we are?"

Sprenkel hadn't noticed. He glanced down.

Two hundred feet, easy. Maybe more. It was hard to tell in the twilight.

"Can't help that!" he shouted in reply. "We've got to bring him down somehow!"

"Well, let's get him over the river!" Levesque shouted. "If we gotta crash, we want to crash over water!"

That made sense. *That's Clinton's destination, anyway.*

"Right! Let's do it! Swing together!"

Their first, ragged attempts at unison swinging eventually transformed into something resembling concerted action. Clinton was forced to overcompensate, causing even wilder swings from the little aircraft.

They were over the water now. Clinton aimed his ultralight toward the Old River dam. Sprenkel realized the man intended to crash into the structure, presumably setting off the explosives as he crashed. It would mean almost certain death, and not only for Clinton.

There seemed to be only one course of action, but they were still too high to attempt it.

He waited, as patiently as he could, forcing down the panic that was rising in his throat.

The ultralight kept descending, and Sprenkel's panic continued to rise.

They were at about a hundred feet now. Still too high. And the dam was approaching rapidly. It would not do to be aboard the aircraft when it met the dam.

He could see Levesque's worried look. He knew what his deputy was thinking, but he shook his head.

Not yet. A little longer.

Seventy-five feet?

Closer, but still too high. A man could be killed if he hit the water wrong at that height.

Seventy-three?

Why doesn't he drop lower? At this height he'll miss the dam entirely.

The ultralight continued dropping lower.

Seventy feet, Sprenkel estimated.

Sixty-five? Sixty feet? The ultralight leveled off as Clinton regained a measure of control. Sprenkel was presented, suddenly, with a frightening revelation.

Clinton wants *to die!*

Of course! He had been imaging the man dropping his explosives like a dive bomber, but that, apparently, was not Clinton's intention.

He has no interest in surviving this mission. There is nothing left for him now. He intends to collide with the dam himself.

Sprenkel made a sudden decision.

"Now!" he shouted to Levesque. "Right now!"

He saw Levesque's puzzled look.

"But what about you? You can't…"

"Don't argue! I'll be right behind you. Just do it!"

Levesque let go. Sprenkel saw him drop into the water. The sudden shift in weight caused the ultralight to swing wildly upward while Clinton tried desperately to regain control. Sprenkel fought to maintain his grip but realized that the effort was futile.

Now or never, he thought, and let go.

He had braced himself for cold, but the water was actually warm. It was August, he realized, but he was nonetheless surprised. The shock of hitting the water took his breath away momentarily, but he rose to the surface and forced himself to swim—laboriously—to the river bank.

Levesque met him on shore with a big grin.

"Pushing your luck, weren't you?" he said, as he hauled Sprenkel out of the water.

"That was a little close, don't you think?"

Sprenkel flopped on the riverbank.

"Had to do it," he said. "Couldn't let him set off those explosives."

"Well, it worked. He crashed over there in that field off to our right. The explosives didn't go off, either."

"We'd better make sure he doesn't get away."

"I'll check it out, but I don't think he's going anywhere. There's been no sign of movement over there. I'd bet he's a dead man."

NATCHEZ, MISSISSIPPI

TWO DAYS LATER

Jasparow had asked for a report on the outcome of the investigation, and Sprenkel had been all too happy to provide it.

They sat in Jasparow's quiet study, where Sprenkel always felt chilled. Perhaps it was the air conditioning; perhaps it was the darkness. Jasparow always had the shades drawn and the lights dim, which made Sprenkel feel as if he were sitting in a refrigerator. Everybody in the South seemed to set their air conditioners at 'sub-zero.' He glanced at Jill, seated beside him, to see whether she felt as cold as he did. He noted with some shock that she was perspiring.

"So, as Abe Lincoln said, the Father of Waters still flows unvexed to the sea," Jasparow said.

"Unvexed to the sea. That's true," Sprenkel said. "And I hope that continues to be the case."

"Don't put too much faith in that," Jasparow replied. "If the river decides it prefers the Atchafalaya channel instead of its own, it will change course in spite of everything we do to prevent it. Nothing remains the same forever."

"Also true," Sprenkel said. "We keep looking for a permanent solution to our problems, but we keep coming up with temporary patchwork solutions, instead. One patch after another."

"Did it ever occur to you that patchwork solutions are the *only* solutions available to us?" Jasparow said. "That there are no permanent solutions? To *any* of our problems?"

"I think I sense a sermon in the making," Sprenkel said.

"Perhaps a small one," Jasparow said with a smile. "You know, Jesus warned us not to get too wrapped up in earthly matters. Remember—don't store up your wealth on earth, where moths and rust can corrupt them, and thieves can break in and steal them. And so on."

"So you're saying," Jill said, "that we shouldn't tinker with the natural order of things? That's just what Harriet's brother was saying."

"That's *not* what I'm saying," Jasparow replied. "Tinkering with nature is our God-given right. In fact, it's not simply a right—it's a necessity. Once you *begin* tinkering with nature, you're going to have to *continue* tinkering with nature."

"Why?" Jill asked.

"To fix the mistakes we made the last time we tinkered with nature," Jasparow said.

"Why is that?"

"Because we're not God. Because we can't predict the future. We can't see all the angles, all the ramifications of what we're doing. Something we haven't taken into consideration is always going to pop up and bite us—pardon the expression—in the ass."

"Hubris," Sprenkel said.

"That's one word for it. I prefer a different term. Original sin."

"Original *sin*?" Jill said.

"That's right," Jasparow said. "Back in the Garden of Eden, people tried to make their own decisions. So God said, 'okay, go ahead. But you're on your own, and you can't change your mind when things go wrong. You can't turn back; Eden is now officially off-limits.'"

"Adam and Eve are just a story," Jill said. "That didn't really happen."

"Maybe not. Maybe it's just a story, but it's a wise and *truthful* story."

"That's a little harsh, don't you think? Why would God make a rule like that, if He loves us?" Jill said.

"I'm not God," Jasparow said. "I'm just a small-time pulpit pounder, so I don't know the answer. But I *am* a father, and I know how tiresome it gets when I have to keep cleaning up the messes my kids make—especially when it's the same sort of mess, over and over and over."

"So God is *tired*?" Jill said.

"That's my guess," Jasparow said. "Or just fed up. When you read the Bible, you see all these stories about God bailing out the human race and chastising His people for the error of their ways. There's the Hebrews in the wilderness making and worshipping that golden calf, Noah and the flood, Sodom and Gomorrah, Job, the Babylonian captivity—the list just goes on and on. And then there's that crucifixion thing. The history of mankind would make *anyone* tired."

"Even God?"

"Even God. Maybe *especially* God."

He thought for a minute.

"There's another possibility, too. Maybe this is God's way of telling us to grow up. Maybe he's kicking us out of the house, hoping to bring us to our senses."

"A little tough love," Sprenkel said.

"Precisely. A little tough love. Maybe that's just what we need."

Jasparow stood and opened his study door.

"I've got a committee meeting in a few minutes, so I'm afraid I'll have to end our meeting now. Thanks for bringing me up to date."

"I'm curious," Sprenkel said as they filed out of the study. "What would your church hierarchy say if they heard your theory that God is tired?"

"Just guessing, of course," Jasparow said, "but I think they'd say 'Here's your hat. Don't let the door hit you on your way out.'"

"In other words, they'd fire you," Sprenkel said.

"It's still just a guess," the minister said, with an ironic smile. "But I think it's a pretty good guess."

As Sprenkel left the church, Jill fell in alongside.

"There's something I need to tell you," she said. "I was coming over to tell you when I saw you leave with Clinton, in that little helicopter."

"His skeeter, yes."

"Well, I went to Baton Rouge the other day. I'd been meaning to get down there and check on the records of this Madeleine Enterprises corporation."

"The company that had been buying up all that land around Morgan City?"

"Right. And I learned there were only two people listed as corporate officers. One was Roger Van Dorn. He was CEO."

"And the other?"

"Edward Clinton. He was vice president and Chief Operating Officer."

"The son?"

"The very one. The name didn't mean anything to me at first, until I was in my car on the way back to Natchez. That's when I remembered the name from the high school yearbook."

"So Clinton must have known the whole story, about the land purchases and everything."

"I think so. I didn't see his name on any of the land purchase documents, but his signature was on the corporate registration forms."

"Which means he was the surviving officer of the corporation. And the holder of all those land options. And if the river changed course, it would flood Morgan City…"

"Right," Jill said. "And those port facilities…"

"And all those port facilities for the petroleum industry would be forced to move upstream," Sprenkel said. "And that land is controlled by…"

"Madeleine Enterprises," Jill said.

"Clinton would have been the surviving officer, sitting on a pot full of money. Neat."

"Of course, the oil companies could always decide to go elsewhere, but where could they go?" Jill said. "With New Orleans ruined as a port and Houston already at capacity, they wouldn't have a choice."

"So all that rhetoric about not tampering with nature was just a smokescreen," Sprenkel said. "Why am I not surprised at that?"

"Because you're just a cynic," Jill said. "A jaded, misanthropic pessimist."

"I guess I am," Sprenkel said. "I'm a cop—it comes with the badge."

"So, what's next for you?" Jill said after giving him a suitable pause for reflection.

"What do you mean?" Sprenkel said.

"I'd think you've earned a little time off, after all this. A day or two, at least."

"I don't think so. This is my job, after all."

"Oh."

"You don't get extra rewards for doing your job, in my experience. That's what the paycheck is for."

"Oh, well…"

"And I've had to put off some things lately, in order to get *this* done."

"Don't you get weekends off, at least?"

"I try to wind down a little on weekends, when it's possible. It isn't always possible."

"What about this coming weekend?" she said.

"I think I'm going to be busy. I'm being evicted from my apartment, so I've got to find a new place by the end of the month."

Jill thought about this.

"I think I've got the solution to your problem," she said finally. "You need a place to live…"

"Right."

"And I need a roommate to help me with the rent. My roommate, you may recall, will not be returning."

"I don't know," Sprenkel said. "This could get a little sticky."

"Why would it be sticky? I'm talking about a simple rent-sharing arrangement. It's not like we're lovers, or anything."

"True."

"Although…"

"Although what?"

"Although we *might* be… you know… if things worked out."

"And if they don't?"

"Well," she said. "*Then* I guess you'd have to look for another place to live. But you'd have some time to look around."

"You make a powerful argument, Ms. Winston."

"I thought so. Do we have a deal?"

Sprenkel made a show of considering her offer, but he knew he would say yes. He had apprehensions about the arrangement, but the idea of living with a beautiful woman—even platonically—was too intriguing to pass up.

"We have a deal," he said.

"Oh, good," she said. "If you like, I'll help you move in. When would you like to start the move?"

"How about this coming Saturday? With as little stuff as I have, it shouldn't take more than a couple of hours."

"Great!" she said. "I'll get the room ready for you. Call me if you need me to help you move."

Jill smiled and turned away toward her car. Then she turned back to him, stepped close and favored him with a hug.

"See you Saturday?" she said.

"I'll be there," he replied, with a smile.

Things are looking brighter, he thought. *I hope I don't screw it up.*

She began walking to her car but turned back to him.

"If Eddie Clinton stood to reap a fortune from this affair, why would he give up and kill himself?" she asked.

Sprenkel shook his head. "I don't know. Although once it was known that he was behind it all, he would have had a hard time taking advantage of it."

"But I've heard you say anything can happen in a courtroom. He might win his case, in spite of the evidence. Wouldn't it be worth taking a chance?"

"I don't know that, either," Sprenkel said, again. "Maybe he was tired of the whole thing."

Jill nodded.

"Like God, you mean?"

"Yes," he said. "Just like God."

* * * *

Tough love. Maybe, thought Sprenkel, that's what God is employing.

Sprenkel wasn't sure how he felt about God, or what he believed. One thing, however, seemed certain: if God existed, John Sprenkel would not be on His list of favorite people. If, in fact, marital fidelity was high on God's list of virtues, then he, Sheriff John Sprenkel, was already probably consigned to hell.

In his youth, that knowledge might have worried him. Now it paled in importance compared to any number of other matters. The earth and its people just kept piling up new offenses at a prodigious rate. If Sprenkel was indeed bound for hell, he suspected he would personally know many of the people there.

I'd be among friends, he thought, wryly. In any event, he couldn't work up any anxiety over the matter. There were too many other, more serious matters to concern himself about.

Before crossing the bridge on his way back to Louisiana, he parked his car near the riverbank. He had always been fascinated by rivers, and the Mississippi fascinated him more than any other. It flowed implacably, relentlessly, to the Gulf of Mexico, despite all the machinations of men. It hard to imagine this mighty stream could be seriously affected by human activities.

But as he stood at the riverside and watched the water moving inexorably to the south, he felt the ground giving way beneath his feet. After stepping quickly backward, he saw a portion of the soil he had been standing on crumble and fall into the stream.

Standing now on (relatively) solid ground, he watched the sod get swallowed by the current. The clump submerged for a bit but then popped back to the surface, already dismembered and broken into smaller pieces. The current swept it on downstream until Sprenkel lost sight of it.

After a moment, he shook his head to chase away the image. He returned to his car and began the drive across the river to his office. He drove uncharacteristically slowly, lost in thought.

AFTERWORD

The story of the Mississippi River and man's relationship to it has been written about extensively. John McPhee described the workings of the Old River Control Structure in his book, *The Control of Nature*. John M. Barry's book, *Rising Tide: The Great Mississippi Flood of 1927 and How It Changed America* (Simon & Schuster, 1997) tells the story of the great flood of that year. I relied also on a contemporary eyewitness account by Lyle Saxon in *Father Mississippi* (The Century Co., 1927). They make fascinating reading.

In addition to relying on various government and academic reports and news accounts, New Orleans native Henry J. Singer, formerly with the Corps of Engineers, read my manuscript and corrected some of my more obvious errors. Any errors that might still exist are, in short, entirely my own fault.

Since this is a work of fiction, a number of real historical figures appear in fictionalized form: Henry Miller Shreve, Nicholas Roosevelt and his young wife Lydia, lawyer A. L. Duncan, and their mutual *bête noir*, Edward Livingston. I've attempted to make my characterizations of them factually correct, while maintaining the fiction writer's prerogative of putting words in their mouths. All other characters, particularly the contemporary characters, are figments of my imagination, including the fictional employees of the very real sheriff's department of Concordia Parish, Louisiana.

And one final note: there is no Natchez University in Natchez, Mississippi. I made that up. Although, now that I think of it, it's not a bad idea at that.

—Clyde Linsley
July, 2014

www.ingramcontent.com/pod-product-compliance
Lightning Source LLC
Chambersburg PA
CBHW050743250626
47155CB00005B/1901